LIGHTS OUT

A Novel

Best wishes and enjoy the ride!

Richard DeVeau

Richard

Library and Archives Canada Cataloguing in Publication
DeVeau, Richard, author
Lights Out / Richard DeVeau

Issued in print and electronic formats.

ISBN: 978-1-998501-17-5 (paperback)
ISBN: 978-1-998501-18-2 (ebook)

Cover Design: Leif Halton
Cover Illustration: Steve Sherrell
Interior Design: Muhammad Tahir

Warpath Press
Toronto, Ontario, Canada
www.warpathpress.com

To Jennie—my heart, my partner, and my biggest fan.

"God saw that the light was good, and he separated the light from the darkness."

Genesis 1:4

Chapter 1

He looked like any other tourist. Or to be more precise, like any other sport fisherman you'd see driving north on Route 42 in Door County in late October.

His pickup truck's camping cap enclosed the back cargo bay, dark-tinted windows reflected the passing landscape. An olive green, twenty-foot aluminum outboard motorboat rocked and bounced on its trailer. His straight-out-of-an-L.L.Bean-catalog outfit, right down to the multi-pocketed fishing vest and wide-brimmed hat with lures and flies hooked into the band, completed the ruse.

Since he never listened to the radio, no matter how long the drive, his phone's GPS broke the silence and told him to take a right onto Isle View Road and head east. As the movie in his mind's eye played a loop of his task and all its possible contingencies, he barely noticed the maples, birches and oaks scantily dressed in pale, late-autumn reds, yellows and browns. He paid no attention to the scuffling rustle of dried leaves his truck kicked up in its wake. The dimming sky barely reflected the letters of the road sign for Europe Bay Woods State Park and he turned on the truck's headlights.

After the GPS told him to take a left onto Northern Door Road, he plucked his phone from the console cup holder and powered it off. To his right, Lake Michigan peeked and glinted through the nearly bare trees. Taking one hand off the wheel at a time, he wiped his clammy palms on a pant leg.

Searching house numbers on this sparsely populated, heavily wooded road, his heart rate picked up. At the correct mailbox, he took a deep breath and exhaled as he headed into the long, winding driveway that ended in a large circle in front of a meticulously manicured fieldstone colonial, past the front door and parked near the attached three-car garage to the left.

After pulling on a pair of rubber surgical gloves, he reached under his seat for a Beretta M96, removed the thread protector from the barrel and screwed on the silencer, nearly doubling the eight-inch gun's length. He racked the slide, putting the first of twelve forty-caliber rounds into the chamber. As he got out of the truck, he slipped the weapon into his belt in the middle of his back and then reached for a map in the driver door's pocket.

Heading quickly toward the door, yellow light from the windows spilled onto the gray paving-stone driveway, a slight breeze carried the earthy scent of decaying leaves, he unfurled the map and pressed the doorbell.

He figured it would be Mrs. Abrams who would answer, and he was right. As she opened the door, a quizzical look on her face, he smiled his broadest smile and said, "I hate to bother you, but I appear to be quite lost and hope you can help me."

A deep man's voice echoed from somewhere down the hallway, "Who is it, Marilyn?"

"A lost fisherman."

As Mr. Abrams appeared from a doorway on the left and headed toward them holding an open newspaper in one hand, his reading glasses in the other, he said, "A fisherman you sa-"

Before he could finish his sentence, a hole appeared in his forehead, red mist exhausted from the back of his head as his body heaped to the floor. As the realization hit her fully, but before the scream could leave her lungs, one appeared in Mrs. Abrams' forehead as well, splattering blood, brain and bone onto the pale beige wall directly behind her.

He pushed her falling body back and quickly entered the house, closing the door behind him with his foot as he dropped the map to put both hands around his weapon and stood still. Smelling dinner's sautéed onions, his stomach growled. Other than the ticking grandfather clock at the other end of the lengthy hallway, he heard nothing else. He went throughout the entire house checking each of its ten rooms, starting with the first floor and then upstairs. As he expected, the house was empty. He knew the Abrams lived alone.

In fact, even though he had never met them before or for that matter had ever been to this Wisconsin peninsula that pierces the northwest side of Lake Michigan like a fat, lowercase letter i, he knew everything there was to know about the Abrams.

Both fifty-eight years old. Married for thirty years. No children. He was a Chicago ad agency executive who had done well building up and then selling his agency to a French communications conglomerate, enabling him to retire early.

She had risen to the position of chief creative officer at another global ad agency, working out of their Chicago office, and continued for three more years before joining her husband in retirement. Although she still loved the thrill of taking on the occasional freelance project and taught an online creative writing course at the University of Wisconsin.

Nothing about them or their lives or their past would give any indication that this was the way they would die. They were merely unfortunate collateral damage, a means to a much greater end. Geography actually killed them— the location of house sealed their fate.

Once down the stairs and back into the hallway, he stepped around Mr. Abram's body, carefully avoiding the expanding pool of blood. He retrieved and refolded his map and stuck it in a vest pocket as he entered the living room. Plopping onto the sofa, he placed his gun next to him and pulled out a second phone, opened its back and inserted the battery. He swiped his apps, scrolled to Twitter and typed, "The lake is peaceful this time of the year. Will fish be biting tonight?" He left the phone on the cushion, headed into the kitchen.

He returned with a ham and cheese sandwich on a plate and a glass bottle of Perrier as his phone chimed. Placing these items on the coffee table in front of him, the Tweet read, "A cleansing rain is expected at the lake." He powered it off, removed the battery, tucked them into a vest pocket, took a large bite of the sandwich and a big pull of sparkling water.

* * *

Captain Dunn watched the setting sun paint bulbous, slate-gray clouds with lucid shades of violet, pink and orange as he deeply inhaled the lake's familiar scent—part wind, part fog, part fish.

Even though he had been making the same run between Canada and Chicago for nearly thirty years, he never tired of views like this from the bridge of his oil tanker. He knew every square inch of Lake Michigan almost better than the freckles on his wife's nose. But he never allowed the familiarity to tempt him into complacency.

He knew all too well that Lake Michigan can be just as dangerous as the open ocean in a storm. Navigating it in any sized vessel demands respect and vigilance. He had faced gale-force winds blowing twenty-four-foot waves across his bow, pummeling his ship with its sixty-pounds-per-square-foot fists. The lake almost claimed his one-thousand-foot freighter as quickly and as fatally as the ocean would have. He and his crew nearly joined the thirty-thousand sailors and their six thousand ships already locked in the lake's eternal embrace. He was fully aware of just how close he came to becoming the inspiration for another Gordon Lightfoot ballad.

His oil laker, the *Blue Nexus*, was carrying more than eighty thousand gallons of dyed diesel fuel in its tanks, heating oil headed to Chicago homes and businesses to buffer the approaching winter. This was the Captain's tenth vessel to command. Over his career he'd served on ships hauling limestone, iron ore, corn, coal, sand and salt to nearly every one of the sixty-three ports that dot this Great Lake.

He had the oil pumped into the ship's six tanks at a port in Ontario. While in port, his seasoned twenty-man crew took care of the transfer operation, taking on eighty-three-thousand gallons of oil without spilling a drop, as well as refueling and restocking the vessel with the food and supplies they'd need for the next two weeks.

It was here in Ontario that something extra was surreptitiously added to his ship, something that he knew nothing about—a small GPS transmitting unit was attached to the mid-ship hull.

* * *

After finishing the sandwich and water, he went through the house collecting whatever valuables he could find, placing them on the couch, including Mr. Abram's wallet, two Rolex watches he found on the bedroom bureau, all of Mrs. Abram's jewelry, a silver tea set that was on the dining room table, a couple of bronze sculptures that looked valuable, and he cut what looked like a Picasso painting out of its frame and rolled it up.

He carried all of these items, and his plate and water bottle, outside, and tossed everything into the boat's bow. He opened the truck's tailgate, removed a five-foot long, two-and-a-half foot wide, two-foot deep, green, military-grade case and carefully placed it in the middle of the boat behind the center steering console.

He went through the house one last time making certain he didn't forget anything or leave any obvious evidence. Satisfied that all was in order, he closed the front door behind him, and drove the pickup around to the back of the house, which faced the lake. He backed the truck and trailer down the Abram's boat ramp, which ran alongside a thirty-foot wooden dock. To the left of the dock, nothing but acres of dark woods against a darkening sky as far as the eye could see—the Abram's property bordered Newport State Forest.

Once the trailer and boat were partially in the water, he got out, went to the trailer, turned the clicking hand winch to the right until the boat floated free, unlatched the cable line, and in one graceful motion shoved off with one foot and jumped in.

He clambered to the center steering console, brought the burbling Mercury to life, pushed the throttle lever to full as he turned the boat 180-degrees and headed east. He left the running lights off, the dark green boat nearly invisible in the moonless night as it sliced through the cold, black water.

The three-mile path to Pilot Island was clearly marked by the steady sweeping beat of the lighthouse's beam. Twenty minutes later, the boat tied to the island's dock, he lifted the military crate, slid it onto the dock and hopped out after it. He pulled a headband flashlight out of one of his vest pockets, stretched the rubber strap over his head and switched it on. Picking up the case with his left hand, leaning against its weight, he pulled his still-silenced Beretta from his belt. At the end of the dock, a crushed-stone path led up a slight hill to the lighthouse, twenty yards away.

He knew it had been automated more than fifty years ago and was now unmanned, like nearly every other operational lighthouse today, and he didn't anticipate anyone being there. But he was taught, "Ready always. Assume nothing."

Once he got to the door, he went to work on the lock with a pick set he pulled from a vest pocket. Just under two minutes later he opened the door and entered with his gun ready, the light from his headlamp inline with his pointed weapon. He quickly determined that the house was indeed unoccupied, confirmed by the layers of dust he illuminated everywhere he turned, by the entombed silence, and the powerful musty smell of moldy, long-undisturbed dampness. He put the gun into his belt as he went back outside to retrieve the case and close the door.

The light tower was at the other end of the room where he proceeded to climb the winding spiral staircase. Even using both hands, the strain of his more than one-hundred-pound load increased as he went and he bumped the case against the wall a few times.

He entered the service room, just below the lantern room, stepped through the door onto the metal grated, railed deck and stopped mid-step, noticing that wherever his light hit the grate and railing, he saw more rust than metal. Gingerly bouncing and testing it with his weight, he then slowly stepped to the left a few more feet so that he was facing the wide-open lake to the east, then gently put the case down with a grunt of relief. After stretching his back, he turned off his headlamp, since the light spilling from the beam spinning fifteen feet above his head provided plenty of illumination.

He kneeled and opened the case, removed an FGM-148 Javelin anti-tank missile launcher, lifted the ranging sight assembly box from it's perfectly-shaped foam rubber bed and attached it to the tube of the shoulder-launched weapon. He then carefully removed one of the two missiles, inserted it into the launch tube and then placed the weapon onto the deck.

He sat down next to the launcher, facing the lake with his back against the lighthouse, reached into his vest for his phone, put the screen in dark mode, scrolled and opened a map of Lake Michigan with a small blinking red dot moving slowly from north to south. It was ten miles away, a half-hour wait, so he exited the map, opened Angry Birds and began to play with the sound off.

* * *

Captain Dunn was in the pilothouse checking course settings once again with his pilot at the helm, Jim Baker. Jim and the captain have been serving together for more than twenty years. There's no better pilot to be found in all five Great Lakes as far as the Captain was concerned. And no better friend. He said, "Looks like we're gonna' have a week of good weather, Jim."

Without turning around, Jim replied, "NOAA says clear skies for most of the next two weeks. We'll see. NOAA isn't God."

"Well, *they* think they are."

"Someone should tell 'em they only forecast the weather, they don't make it."

"Sure. But do we ever move without consulting them? Kinda makes them at least god-like. God adjacent?"

Noting the south by slightly southwest heading, and before turning and stepping through the open door onto the stern deck, Dunn started singing. "NOAA loves me, this I know. Cuz' their weather reports tell me so."

"You're off key and a bit pitchy."

The Captain usually relaxed at this point in the journey. This was one of the most open and deepest parts of the lake. The ship had just crossed the border of Michigan and was now in Wisconsin waters, although the difference was merely a dotted line on a map.

As the twin V-16 diesel engines turned the screws at near full speed, the vast vessel moved at eighteen knots, about twenty miles an hour, across the relatively calm lake. He could see a few small lights from houses several miles away on the shore off his starboard side. In the distance to the south and east, the sweeping light of the Pilot Island lighthouse was growing brighter as he got closer, although five miles away was the closest he'd get.

Pilot Island was one of fifty lighthouses operating along the lake's shores and inlets that he had come to know so well. Logically, lighthouses were inanimate objects, but emotionally they had become living beings with pulsing heartbeats of light. Though no longer really needed in today's satellite-saturated, GPS-guided world, he loved their history and the important role they played in aiding and comforting sea and lake-faring folk like him.

A nautical traditionalist, Dunn was ardent about keeping with his trade's long-standing practice of giving everything seaworthy and sea-related a female name. Because the location of Pilot Island was a few miles offshore and surrounded by state forest, making its light very bright against the dense, mostly unpopulated blackness, Dunn thought of it as a striking, bold, confident woman—much like his own adult daughters. So in honor of his oldest, he had named this lighthouse, Liz. He named others after the rest of his daughters, his wife, mother, and mother-in-law. Some he named after historical women he admired and others were names he simply liked.

After making an observational three-hundred and sixty-degree turn, he stepped through the pilot house door to get another cup of coffee.

* * *

His app indicated that the ship was just about at the desired location, so he powered the phone off and picked up the missile launcher and placed it onto his right shoulder. Peering into the sight, he set it for night vision, pressed the power button, starting a low-buzzing hum of electronics and lighting up the targeting box and range finder, instantly locking onto the ship.

He selected the direct-launch mode option, watched the digital display track the ship for three more seconds, took a deep breath and pulled the trigger.

The four-foot missile shot out of the tube several feet, propelled by its compressed gas cylinder, the main engine ignited a fraction of a second later in a pale-blue burst of solid-fuel-propelled flame, sending the howling missile toward its target at nearly five-hundred feet-per-second.

Captain Dunn was standing on the bridge's deck sipping his coffee when he noticed something odd as he looked toward Pilot Island off to his right—a flaming light seemed to detach itself from the lighthouse, heading toward him at an alarming speed.

Had he known that his life and his crew's would end in the next minute, he probably would have at least been thinking of something other than his last round of golf.

As the realization struck him, wide-eyed, he turned to face the open pilothouse door and said, "Jim, I think we're about to meet NOAA."

* * *

As the missile streaked away, momentarily warming him, he took his eyes off the sight, moved the case closer for easier access to the second missile. The smell of burning lighter fluid and sulfur lingered in the slight breeze.

Like the first, the second missile still in the case was also modified to double its normal three-mile range and it too was armed with an extra nasty, two-phase armor-piercing and incendiary warhead. Both modifications he did himself. He could load the second missile into the tube and be ready to shoot in under twenty seconds.

He preferred to watch with his naked eye rather than through the launcher's electronics, so he pulled a small pair of binoculars from a pocket and watched the missile's glow quickly recede into the blackness. He followed its vivid tail mirrored along the water's surface, waiting just over a minute before the first of six or seven explosions in rapid succession, each one rolling into the next, light up the lake in an expanding, fiery mix of oranges, reds and yellows, jettisoned flaming debris and roiling gray and black smoke as eighty-thousand gallons of burning fuel oil covered and ignited everything that once encased it.

It took only five minutes for the largest of the viciously separated sections of the 925-foot ship to completely disappear into its watery grave and final resting place six hundred feet below. What remained of the eighty-thousand gallons of fuel oil burned on the surface of the lake for almost two days as the wind spread it to an area of more than a quarter of a mile in circumference before dying out.

With one missile more than enough to complete the job, he disassembled the launcher and returned it to its case. Replaced his headlamp and retreated the same way he came. The case noticeably lighter, matching his growing mood. He began whistling Darth Vader's Imperial March as he made his way down the spiral stairs.

He returned to the Abrams'—his return trip not only once again aided by the lighthouse, but also enhanced by the glowing sky from the fire-lit lake—and docked the boat, and returned the missile case to the pickup's bed.

He then untied and turned the boat around so that it faced east again. He started the motor, knelt onto the dock as he reached in for the gas tank and emptied it into the boat. He lit a match, then the matchbook, tossed it in, igniting everything in a dazzling, loud whoosh.

He emptied his still-silenced gun into the boat's floor, tossed the gun in, followed by his rubber gloves, pushed the boat's throttle lever slightly forward with his foot, sending the flaming vessel on its way, like a Viking funeral on steroids. It traveled roughly one hundred yards before finally sinking out of sight and sound.

He returned to his truck, took out his second phone, added the battery, opened Twitter and typed, "Landed the big one. New bait test a huge success!" He then shut the phone off and removed the battery.

He pulled out of the Abram's boat ramp, back along the winding driveway and out into the Wisconsin night.

Chapter 2

Charlene, owner and curator, swept her hand around the vast white-walled, high-ceilinged art gallery peppered with large colorful paintings, her voice echoing as she said, "Well, what do you think?"

"I like it... But..."

"But what?"

As Eve walked over to it, "This painting would look better over there on that wall. I think it's my strongest piece. Should be the first one people see as they walk into the space."

"Okay, Eve. So let it be written, etcetera, etcetera."

"Good, so let's move it now." Eve Tuant dropped her shoulder bag to the floor as she walked over to the six-foot tall, four-foot wide painting in question, removed it from the wall, carried it over to its new location and swapped places with the painting currently there, then did the reverse with the replaced painting.

"There. Much better. Don't you think?"

"Go ahead, twist my arm... yes, yes, you're right. I like it there, too."

Eve smiled and said, "This is our third show together. You should know by now that I'm always right."

"I know you always *think* you're right. What happens to people who disagree with you?"

"The ones who live, you mean?"

"Ha, ha, very funny," is what Charlene said, but not what she was thinking. There was something about Eve that she couldn't put her finger on. Something hard and dark. *Pretty much describes most artists I've known*, as she thought about it. But this was something else. Something deadly. *I don't feel at all threatened. In fact, just the opposite. I feel safe when I'm with her. I just know if it came to it Eve would protect me. Not that I need protection. Nope. I can hold my own, thank you very much. But in my gut, I just know it would be something she would do instinctively, not just for me, but for anyone needing protection.*

The fact that Eve wasn't gay didn't stop Charlene from imagining being with her. Who wouldn't. Eve was gorgeous. *If only I were 20 years younger. But who knows, Eve is French. That she's actually French Canadian doesn't matter. French is French. More open minded about things like having sex with women, even older women. And let's be honest, I look great for my early fifties.* But she learned the hard way years ago not to mix business with pleasure, work with sex, artists with the showing and selling of their art.

As she thought about it, the sense of protection Charlene felt probably had a lot to do with Eve's years in the military. "It was a while," was all she said when Charlene asked. "Army," was all she got when she asked what branch. The fact that she is from and served in Canada came out in another conversation. That she's also a US citizen was revealed in an exchange about sales taxes and Form 990s.

Charlene had been working with Eve Tuent for more than four years now, but other than her name, where she lived, and the obvious fact that she's a fabulous painter who did some sort of consulting work with the Boston police is pretty much the extent of what she knows.

Eve continued, "I do love how the paintings look in here. I never grow tired of the feeling I get when I see the work on a gallery's walls. They seem to have, I don't know, more weight than they do when they're in my studio. It's like they hold more space, have more volume, more gravitas."

"Well, they do. The work's on stage. This is art theatre, darling. Each painting a star. And so are you. Did I mention that nearly half of these have sold already?"

"Half? Really?"

"Really. And the opening is still a week away. I've yet to put red dots on the pieces that have sold, but that'll be done before the opening, for sure. I hope you're working on some new ones. I want to add another exhibit for you into the schedule as soon as I can. And I want to include a couple of your new pieces in a group show in four months."

Eve smiled and nodded, "Wonderful" was all she said. Eve couldn't tell Charlene that she was not going to be painting as much as she had been. Couldn't tell her that she would be spending a lot more time working with the Boston Office of

Homeland Security team over the next several months, getting to know every tea-stained square foot of Boston harbor.

And she certainly couldn't tell her why.

Chapter 3

The police station in District D-4 is in Boston's South End, on Harrison Ave., a convenient five-block walk from Eve's studio loft apartment. In the opposite direction, she was only two blocks away from Charlene's Newbury Art Gallery. She chose this location exactly for the proximity to both, and she was quite lucky to acquire a studio in the highly desirable Lamont Lofts building, and on the fifth and top floor, no less. The fact that Homeland Security had a heavy hand in moving Eve to the front of the waitlist for her loft had everything to do with her "luck."

As Eve entered the station's main conference room, she noticed that this month's Homeland meeting had the usual players—Captain Bill Evans, the station's commanding officer, senior detectives and partners, Dick Sweeney and Dick Murphy, who are quick to tell anyone they meet that when it comes to police work, two Dicks are always better than one, Boston FBI's Special Agent in Charge (SAC), Joe Bonnato—and someone new.

"There she is," Bill said, stirring his cup as he turned from the credenza holding the coffee pot, stacks of paper cups, a tray of plastic stirrers, and some napkins beside a box of donuts, cliché be damned. Tossing the brown plastic stick into the trash can, he added, "Eve, do you know Hunter Forte? He's also with Homeland."

"No, we've not met."

Standing up from his seat at the far end of the glass-topped conference table, walking two steps and reaching his hand out over the table, Hunter said, "Nice to meet you."

"Ditto." As they shook hands, she asked, "What division are you with?"

"I'm with CWMD."

Dick Sweeney piped in, "For us unwashed and unworthy of the federal hoi polloi, what's CWMD?"

As she placed her laptop bag onto the table and hung her coat on the back of her chair, Eve answered, "It's a division created a couple of years ago, Countering Weapons of Mass Destruction."

Smiling, Sweeney said, "Oh sure, I heard of it. Saddam Hussein is president emeritus, right?"

His partner, Dick Murphy, said, "You should know. Dey found him in *youah* basement."

"Yeah, but he was with *your* mother."

Captain Evans spoke as he went to a whiteboard wall with a large map of the city of Boston and the harbor, "Alright gang, we've got a lot to cover today, so let's get started, okay?"

Chapter 4

His passport said he was Peter Holt, but his fingerprints and DNA said that was a lie. His perfectly forged passport and credit card were all the truth the airline needed to book his flight from Chicago to Boston and to breeze through O'Hare's security check, even with all of its shoe-and-clothing removing, scanning, conveyor-belt recovery and re-dressing nonsense.

After tying his shoes, he picked up his knapsack and began heading toward his gate, slipping into the stream of humanity moving swiftly in both directions of the cavernous terminal. Slowing to gaze in awe at the four-story tall, 72-foot long Brachiosaurus skeleton that stands guard at Terminal One, he noticed a McDonalds near his gate and headed over for a bacon, egg and cheese biscuit and bottle of water.

Peter had dropped off the pickup truck and empty boat trailer at the prearranged used-car lot in Northern Illinois two nights after the Wisconsin phase of the plan was completed with such awe-inspiring success. The missile launcher and unused missile had been removed from the truck the night before, quickly transferred to another vehicle in the dark parking lot of the hole-in-the-wall

Wisconsin motel he had booked for just that reason. He also tossed the clothes he wore, his fishing vest, boots and hat into the motel's dumpster.

Since it was after midnight, the car lot's office and the street it was on were empty and still. He left the keys under the truck's seat as instructed, wiped down the steering wheel and everything else he may have touched, and walked over to a white Honda Accord parked nearby, tossed his small suitcase and knapsack into the back seat, retrieved the key from behind the driver's-side visor and drove off the lot, headed for O'Hare airport.

He booked a room at the Hilton at O'Hare for the night. While its four-stars are nice, it's literally in the middle of the airport and a quick walk to the terminal. He parked the Honda in the long-term lot, thinking, *I guess "forever" is as long a term as it gets*, since he was never coming back for it and a trace for its owner would lead nowhere.

Peter settled into his room on the fifth floor with a view of the airport's control tower. Too late to order room service and the hotel's three restaurants were long closed, he selected a number of snacks from the minibar and a bottle of water and started in on a bag of fruit and nut mix.

He wiped his salty hand on his pant leg and sent a quick text on his phone. Then pulled a second phone from his pocket, inserted the battery, opened Twitter and typed, "Midwestern birds successfully migrated south. Some head east?" Minutes later his phone pinged and he saw the Tweet he was looking for, "Northern New Hampshire is beautiful this time of year!"

After reversing the battery procedure, Peter tossed the phone into his backpack. He then dropped his regular phone, the snacks and water onto the bed. Picked up the TV remote and flipped through stations until he got to CNN. He kicked off his shoes and stretched out on the bed, added a couple of extra pillows, leaned back and continued eating as he watched.

As he suspected, the dramatic explosion and sinking of the oil tanker was pretty big national and, most likely, international news. Helicopter footage shot earlier today showed the still-burning oil slick. Strewn in the midst of the flames were varying sizes and shapes of mostly unidentifiable floating and smoldering debris.

Pictures of the ship's captain and crew scrolled across the screen as the news anchor called the violent sinking of the *Blue Nexus* a tragic and unprecedented accident that authorities were just beginning to investigate. He muttered, "Good luck." as he opened his phone's browser and did a search for Wisconsin news, narrowed his selection to Door County. As he suspected, nothing about the Abrams was mentioned yet.

That wouldn't happen for another two weeks.

The mailman, coming to the Abram's house to deliver a package that needed a signature, rang the bell and waited. The unmistakable pong of decomposing flesh that wafted through the edges of the front door assaulted and shocked his senses. Dropping the package, he stumbled backwards a few steps, reached for the cell attached to his belt and made a 911 call.

Chapter 5

The meeting had been going on for about half an hour, mostly recapping the progress the team has made thus far, when Hunter Forte spoke up. "This is probably a good time to cover why I'm here. Most of you may know about Homeland's Securing The Cities Program, created and focused on detecting and preventing radiological and nuclear terrorist attacks. STC provides select cities with thirty-million dollars plus equipment, training and support. Boston'll be added to the program. I'm here for the next year or so to help you prepare and get up and running smoothly."

Eve asked, "What about threats that are not nuclear or radiological, will the program cover those?"

"Nukes and dirty bombs are top priority obviously, but the procedures and resources that STC establishes could easily be employed in any large-scale attack, nuclear or not. Got something in mind?"

"I'm sure you've all seen the news over the last week or so about the oil freighter exploding on Lake Michigan?"

On their nods and one-word affirmative replies and grunts, she continued, "We don't think it's an accident."

Sweeney asked, "Who's we, Homeland?

Joe Bonnato answered, "Homeland, FBI, NSA, NCIS, ATF and CIA."

"Shit, that's pretty much the entire Fed alphabet soup!"

Eve added, "CIA began catching wind of what could be a sophisticated and coordinated terrorist cell operating here in the states. Some chatter about Boston's been picked up more than once."

"You think they blew up the tanker?"

"Perhaps."

"What the hell for? Sure, it's a tragedy, but apart from the crew and maybe some Lake Michigan fish, the impact's pretty contained."

"Not sure. Coulda' been a trial run of some kind."

"Trial for what, though?"

"Think about it, Dick... what's the most dangerous and potentially deadly non-nuclear cargo that regularly comes into this harbor and three others along the East Coast?"

Murphy went to the map and pointing said, "Gotta be the liquid natural gas. Comes into Everett, right heah, trew the Mystic Rivah outlet heah. There's a buncha storage tanks on the propady, too. And some uddahs on the Chelsea and East Bahstan side."

"Yup. And don't forget the terminal at Commercial Point in Dorchester."

"Shit, yeah, how could I foghet dat? That giant tank sticks out like a sowah thumb. Seen for miles. The rainbow painted on it like a frickin' bull's-eye."

Sweeney, said, "You should feel pretty embarrassed right about now. You just got schooled 'bout your own home town. And by a Canuck, no less!"

"Fuck you, Sweeney."

Smiling, "Love you too, buddy."

Eve continued, "Just so you know, boys, I'm a citizen of both Canada *and* the U.S., so that's Yankee-Doodle Canuck, if you don't mind, eh.

"Under normal conditions, LNG is quite safe. Tankers have been coming in and out of this harbor since 1971 without incident. This is the oldest of the four East Coast LNG ports. But it's also the only one located so close to where people live. You guys don't even need to look at the map. You know all too well that the LNG port is surrounded by tightly packed neighborhoods—triple decker houses, apartment buildings, businesses, offices and schools. Not to mention all the new high-rise office and apartment buildings that just went up on the Somerville and Everett line.

"LNG is basically methane cooled to two-hundred-an-sixty-degrees below zero. You can drop a lit match into it and nothin'll happen. It's lighter than air, so in a leak or spill it warms quickly, rises and harmlessly dissipates into the air."

"Like cow farts... and mine." Sweeney added.

"She said 'hahmlessly'. Yours peel wallpapa, buddy," Murphy said as he went back to his chair.

Eve went to the map, pointing with her pen as she spoke, "But, if there's a massive leak, a large gas cloud quickly forms and, if ignited, this cloud would burn hot enough to melt steel up to twelve hundred feet away. Anyone living within this mile or so radius would be killed instantly, and everyone in this two-and-a-half mile radius would suffer severe burns, everything combustible catches fire. And because it's so packed, the fire rapidly cascades. Within six minutes, the fire radius expands out here, twelve miles. The Department of Energy did a study on this a number of years ago. They estimated the number of dead and injured would be in the hundreds of thousands."

"H...o...l...y shit," Sweeney whispered. No one else said a word—the looks on all their faces reflecting the gravity of what they just heard.

Murphy broke the silence, "Whada we know?"

Bonnato got up and headed to the coffee pot as he said, "Not a lot concrete yet. A terrorist cell is either forming or already formed and operational on American soil. All U.S. citizens, we believe. And, as Eve said, a couple of mentions of Boston from different sources were picked up in the ether."

Murphy, his hands flailing as he spoke. "You shitin' me? Citizens? Not radicalized towelheads lookin' for a replaya 9/11? What the hell. Ah dey at least in cahoots widda Muslims?"

Eve said, "We don't think so. At least we haven't found a connection to any other country or any other group. Not yet, anyway. Keep in mind that over the last several years, more than half of those charged with terrorism in this country have been U.S. citizens. Either way, it's why we think there may be more to the Lake Michigan oil tanker explosion."

Joe swallowed his last bite of donut, brushed some crumbs from his shirt and continued. "Among other things, we're monitoring social media. We think it's how they communicate. Hidden in plain sight. Or at least they think they're hidden. We just launched a new sophisticated algorithm to sniff around."

Sweeney said, "Be a lot easier if they just posted selfies, wouldn't it?" Holding his cell phone above his head and looking up at it. "Here with my buds and this bomb we just made. Like and follow us! Hashtag, radicalknuckleheads."

Murphy said, "Now you'll needa be more cahful bout sendin' your anonymous dick pics, buddy."

"How's that possible when it's all your wife keeps asking me for?"

Eve, still standing at the map and rapidly clicking her pen, said, "While the Coast Guard, State police and your Harbor Patrol have been escorting every LNG tanker coming into the harbor since 9/11, we in this room need to come up with a plan to augment that protection."

Hunter added, "Great! One of the reasons I'm here."

Eve reached for her coffee cup on the table, drained it and said, "The Guard and Harbor patrol can stop direct, on-the-water threats, but can't do much if the tanker is wired to explode, or hit by a missile. In fact, those providing protection surrounding the ship are most likely among the first casualties."

Captain Evans spoke up, "Normal procedure's been Coast Guard intercepts, boards and inspects each LNG tanker while it is still miles from the Harbor. They don't stop the boat, but do come alongside and board it to conduct a bow-to-stern search for bombs and other potential threats. That said, all of this is why we've kept this group small and contained. It will mean extra work for each of us. And I know this is our sixth meeting, the first for you, Hunter, but I feel it's worth repeating that everything discussed here never leaves this room. You don't tell your spouse, your priest, or your dog. We clear? Whatever shit may be coming our way, our job is to keep it from hitting the fan. Got it?"

Sweeney said, "God help the fuckers who try. We been puttin' anyone with an aim to harm Boston into the ground since 1775."

Murphy added, "Hey, Capn', ain't dat the date on your high school yeahbook?"

"Fuck you, Murphy. The pot's nearly empty, so why don't you make some more coffee and let's all get to work. Sweeney, go grab the easel and some markers out of my office and let's start brainstorming and putting some thoughts on paper. No idea's too crazy. And let's keep our wives and mothers out of it, okay? Gesturing with his pen at Murphy and Sweeney. "Yeah. I'm lookin' at you two."

Chapter 6

The flight from Chicago to Logan was uneventful with the exception of a patch of rough turbulence over Lake Erie that caused what was left of his Sprite to rain on his lap. Peter was now driving the car left for him in the long-term parking lot at the airport. He headed north on Route 93, carefully observing the speed limit, which he would maintain for the entire three-hour drive to his destination. He did consider flying into Manchester and cutting about an hour off the trip, but decided there was greater anonymity among larger numbers of people, so he determined Logan was the better choice, and he actually enjoyed long, quiet drives. Never felt to the need to fill the void with music or news, preferring his own thoughts and musings.

He was heading for a secluded farmhouse in Bethlehem, New Hampshire. While initially built in the early 1800's, the house didn't need much to modernize it for his stay. It was the barn that had the most work done. The barn was the reason he was here. It now has a heat source and all the special tools and supplies needed for the next nine months—the time it will take to enhance four missiles and wait for the warmth of summer.

The temperature will play a vital role in this next phase of his plan.

The one missile he didn't use in Wisconsin was already at the farmhouse and the other three will arrive in a couple of days, securely crated and loudly labeled as fragile glass.

The irony of where he was heading struck him as he crossed the Massachusetts/New Hampshire border. The sign with "Welcome" and "Bienvenue" across the top. At the bottom, the state motto, "Live Free or Die." He had heard or read somewhere that the state was considering dropping the "or die." *I hope they keep it. It's such an on-the-nose New England attitude. Be a shame to quiet such a distinct voice.*

For as many months as a gestating womb, he'll live and work in a town that bears the same name as that of Christ's birth. Peter saw it as a clear and confirming sign that his mission was indeed a holy one. That, like Christ, new life would be birthed out of death. His uncle had convinced him of that.

Over the course of many months of meetings and phone conversations with his uncle, Peter grew certain that the country needed to be reformed and refined by fire. *This country needs redirection. To take back its rightful place on the world stage. The course needs correcting. And demonstrated power is the only way to do it.*

Democracy is failing. It's no longer working, no longer bearing the right fruit. Or any fruit for that matter. Polarization is absolute. There's no longer any ground in the middle. It's been demolished by so many verbal and political grenades lobbed from the left and the right. Not a single square inch remains.

It's time to break the mold. It is only right that this new order have its genesis in the Live-Free-or-Die state. That Peter will play an important role in bringing it about made him proud of his appointed destiny.

Chapter 7

Mitchell loved skating on Lake Michigan in December. This year, the weather followed its normal Door County pattern and the ice is now thick enough to hold his weight, but also still quite transparent, enabling him to see all the way to the lake's bottom. He loved the thrill of gliding over giant boulders nestled among woven patterns of waterlogged trees and leaves nearly twenty-feet below.

Since it hadn't snowed yet and there wasn't much wind at the moment the surface turned solid, he was enjoying a nice, nearly bump-free ride under his freshly sharpened hockey blades.

He turned left around a jutting spruce tree-filled peninsula, heading in long gliding strides toward the Abrams' dock in the center of a cove.

He was away at college when his parents called him with the awful news. As neighbors, he and his parents knew Marilyn and Robert fairly well. They were always kind to him when he was younger. If he was playing in his yard or driveway, they would wave hello and occasionally stop to chat with him and his parents on their daily walk by his house.

And more recently, when the Abrams learned that Mitchell was majoring in art history at the University of

Chicago, they invited him into their home several times to show him their collection of original art—paintings and sculpture that reflected their eclectic tastes that leaned toward postmodern abstraction. He remembered being quite taken back when they showed him their prized possession, an unmistakable Picasso painting.

Seeing the back of their house now as he skated closer brought on a fresh wave of grief, tinged with a bit of fear at the realization that violence and death could be so close by, so intimate, not just some distant, abstract event that happened elsewhere on the daily news.

As he got closer to their dock, something in the ice caught his eye and he abruptly stopped, spraying a wave of shaved ice high into the air.

Slowly gliding toward what he saw, bending over holding his knees, he couldn't believe his eyes. Staring up at him, her white and green geometric face frozen in place an inch below the surface, was the Abrams' Picasso. He could see a round hole in her floppy purple hat, an entire side of the painting's blue background badly burnt. He then noticed just beyond the painting, sitting on the bottom about fifteen feet below, an outboard motor and the boat it was attached to.

With his heart racing, his mind still trying to grasp what he was seeing, he pulled off his glove, got his cell phone out of his coat pocket and dialed 911 and then his parents. He then skated over to the Abram's dock, sat and waited.

Chapter 8

As the meeting broke up, Hunter stepped over to Eve as she put her laptop into its case. "Would you like to go grab a coffee? As the new guy I'm hoping I can pick your brain about a couple of things."

At first Eve almost said no. A knee jerk reaction to constantly being hit on. The fact that Hunter was a new colleague—and it didn't hurt that he was a very attractive one; tall, dark, and lickable, as her cousin was fond of saying about guys she thought were hot—caused her to pause and agree, telling him that her favorite place was only a couple blocks and short walk away on Union Park street.

They exited the police station, took a right and walked rather quickly, huddled into themselves in the cold, not saying much. Five minutes later they were at a small table near the window of a boutique coffee shop, named, *Perkatory.*

After ordering—latte and a blueberry scone for her, cappuccino and slice of apple pie for him—Eve asked, "How long have you been in Boston?"

"About a week."

"Where you staying?"

"Homeland set me up with a place at the Jones Apartments on East Dedham Street."

"Wow, close to the station. Right around the corner."

"Yup, all of three-minutes if I walk slowly. Where are you?"

"Down Harrison a few more blocks. Lamont Lofts."

"Lofts as in artists lofts? On her nod, "I heard you're an artist. A painter, right? I'd love to see your work sometime. I minored in art history in college."

"Friday night. I have a solo show opening. The gallery's a few blocks further down Harrison, on Thayer Street. The Newbury."

"No kidding? I didn't realize you're in the big leagues. A solo gallery exhibit. Wow. Impressive. When do you find time to paint?"

"Whenever I can. I'm only in the station office a couple of days each month. At least up to now. So, if I'm not working on something Homeland or Agency related, I paint on those days for sure. Most nights. Weekends always. I find painting cathartic. Cheap therapy, considering. Although, with the prices of art supplies these days, I'm not so sure that's still the case. I just shelled out eight hundred and fifty bucks for six, sixteen-ounce jars of paint! Who was your favorite artist in college?"

"I had several. Still do. Most of the abstract expressionists. Love de Kooning and Rothko. It took me a while to get there, but the more of Joan Mitchell's work I saw, the bigger a fan I've become. I'm enamored with

Kline. What he did with nothing more than bold strokes of black paint knocks my socks off."

"Well, now I'm a bit intimidated by the thought of you coming to my show. You're certainly no uninformed observer." She was feeling herself warm to him in a way that surprised her. Not only because they had just met, but because it had also been quite some time since she allowed these emotions a foothold. That door was shut. Locked. Sealed. It was almost alarming her to see how quickly her thoughts picked that lock and her feelings cracked open that door. She thought getting back to business would help her find some equilibrium and said, "So what did you want to pick my brain about?"

"Just want your take on the team. Evans and the two Dicks seem like typical cops. Street smart, cop smart. Deeply concerned for the welfare and wellbeing of their community, willing to lay it all on the line. But Bonnato is a bit of a mystery. I know I just met him. And maybe my feelings are skewed because he's with the FBI. I've had my share of scuff-ups with several of his ilk over the years. My working theory is there's something in the water at Quantico."

She took a sip of her latte and said, "You don't need to worry about Bonnato. He's the real deal. Did you know he oversaw the counterterrorism investigation of the Boston Marathon bombings?"

"No, I didn't," he muttered through a mouthful of pie, covering his mouth with his hand.

"That's how we met. How I came to Boston. The Agency sent me here to help in an unofficial/official capacity, if you know what I mean."

"Yup. Got it. CIA and domestic investigations, a potentially slippery, tangled, messy slope that we eventually hear about."

"Not if they're done right." She smiled at that remark and let it hang in the air for a beat.

"Which ones were done right?"

"Exactly."

Stirring some sugar into his cappuccino, "Ah. Good one."

"Anyway, Joe was dogged. Relentless. He grew up here. Took the bombings very personally. He's the one who shot the younger Tsarnaev brother, caused his older brother to run him over with the getaway car."

"No... shit..."

"He also headed up tracking the older brother down. Plucked Tsarnaev from his hiding place in that boat parked in a Watertown resident's driveway. Why he rose so quickly to become the FBI's Boston SAC at a pretty young age. There's no one I'd want on my team more than Joe. He's really good at this. And a good friend. "

"Got it. Thanks. I feel better."

As she looked into his eyes and held them for a moment before returning her attention to her scone, she noticed and sensed that feeling better about Joe Bonnato isn't all he felt. She tried to push those thoughts aside. But that only brought them to the fore.

Not sure I'm ready for another relationship. Or if I'll ever be. After all, who'd really want me beyond a shallow physical fling? I'm damaged goods. They all find out eventually. Or I end it before they can. At least this one isn't an artist. Maybe that will make a difference this time. Or perhaps I'm just too broken for anyone. I know Afghanistan did a number on me. It did a number on most of us.

Is that why I'm so strong and confident, except when it comes to love? When it comes to being emotionally available and vulnerable? Why it's so hard to trust, to be open and transparent with someone who isn't family? Even family sometimes gets a wall. When the hurt is just too great and the reason too painful to share.

It can't be normal to be willing to take a bullet wound over a heart wound any day of the week. Topic for another time. Another shrink perhaps? Nah. Hate opening up to them, too. It's good he isn't an artist. Isn't it? Yeah it is. How many times have I tried to make those work? Talk about insanity.

But this is all very premature, isn't it? We just met, for crying out loud! And there's plenty of other stuff I need to think about and focus on anyway.

But, I must say, it would be real easy to get lost in those pale blue eyes staring at me right now.

Chapter 9

Senator Trahison, leaning back in the chair at his desk, was going over tomorrow's agenda that his secretary just handed to him before she left for the evening. A faint whiff of her perfume lingered on the page. She also emailed it to him, but the senator preferred the tactile touch of paper and the ability to write notes in the margins. Staff meeting at 7:30 a.m., followed by two twenty-minute meetings with key constituents and contributors and then, if there are no calls for floor votes, the rest of the day will be a strategy meeting with his senior team.

They need to stay on top of his bill. As it now heads to the Senate floor for debate and vote, the main strategy, the one they'll spend the most time discussing tomorrow, is centered on attaining unanimous consent agreements from as many senators as possible. These agreements will limit the time available for debating and amending. There's too much at stake.

Bill H.R.7174 is a paradigm changer. It will establish a new Office of Inspector General to Oversee State Spending and Waste. A worthy endeavor that, on paper, looks like the prudent course to follow in light of today's multi-trillion-dollar federal funding machinery.

What the bill will actually do, in "normal" times, is give this new Office significant influence over every state's spending of federal funds. But, when times are not normal, specifically when the President declares a national state of emergency, triggered by another 9/11-like event, the Inspector General's influence over each state's federal money becomes complete control.

There's a clause buried in 7174 that connects it to the Patriot Act, giving this Inspector General absolute authority over all of this money when a new national emergency status is established by Presidential decree.

Once H.R.7174 becomes law, it can either be challenged and eventually struck down by the Supreme Court, amended by Congress, or another law passed to dissolve it. The President could also issue an executive order. By the time any of those steps are taken, if taken at all, it could be months or even years from now. By then the tables will have been turned.

Essentially, this law establishes a parallel government, at least as far as federal money goes. But money is oxygen. Control over who can breathe and who can't is ultimate power. Providing one person with this power is the true goal of H.R.7174.

The bill decrees the selection and appointment of this Inspector General will be determined solely by the head of the Senate Finance Committee. Since that just so happens to be Senator Trahison, he'll become the power behind the power, the hand inside the puppet, the wizard behind the curtain.

Making H.R.7174 law will be the realization of a small but very powerful group's goals, a group that the media could define as a cabal, if they ever caught wind of its existence.

It's the crowning move of this group's long game, an orchestrated strategy to take the most troublesome wild card of governing out of play—the states themselves.

The senator and this cabal are convinced that the original Constitution didn't take federalism far enough, didn't remove enough state power. Especially after the Supreme Court's presumption against preemption decisions made in the New Deal era of the 30s and 40s and all of the muddy decisions made since then regarding express and implied preemption.

He thought, *The degree of federalism currently baked into the Constitution's Sixth Article has served as a check against any states with wildly independent ideologies and rogue tendencies. Thanks to the influence of my hero, Alexander Hamilton. But the Supremacy Clause in Article 6 is no longer keeping pace with today's new world realities. And the courts still aren't getting it right. My bill will now fix these deficits.*

This new law will provide complete financial control over the unpredictable, left-leaning, self-righteous Blue states that the senator despises, especially those on each coast—the states he and others are convinced to be the source of liberal, socialist poison currently infecting the country, especially our impressionable youth.

Conversely, this law gives the Inspector General the power to enhance the impact and influence of the loyal Red states—influence the senator believes with all of his heart they so rightly deserve as they take on the Great Satan, the godless left, in the eternal battle for America's soul.

It took a lot of arm-twisting, cajoling, and not-so-thinly-veiled threats by Senator Trahison to get the bill this far, especially during the rancorous second reading and debate that took place in the House a few weeks ago. It was close. Too close.

H.R.7174 survived the Oversight and Reform Committee, recently passing the House with little damage done, thanks to some timely quid-pro-quo promises and squeezing more than a few pressure points. And now my bill is about to be brought before the Senate to essentially start the process all over again.

The key to moving this through is keeping proposed floor amendments to a minimum. So our work now is getting as many senators as possible to consent to accept limits on their right to debate and offer non-germane amendments. We're gonna continue to work the phones and stalk other key senators at home, in their offices, on the Senate floor and throughout the hallways for the next month. We're so close to achieving unanimity. Vigilance and tenacity are now the keys to the kingdom.

There's no time for the bill to be sent back to the House, which happens if the Senate's changes are significant enough, if too many amendments get attached. Especially amendments that have nothing at all to do with the bill. The longer H.R.7174 remained under scrutiny, the greater the chance its true intent could be discovered.

Which would not only kill the bill, the senator knew it would kill his career and perhaps even end his freedom. *Especially if the Democrats and their belligerent, self-righteous Attorney General have their way with me.*

Time is also compressing for another reason—other vital interconnected wheels are already in motion. Stopping them now is not an option.

As his party's powerful minority leader, and hopefully majority leader once again after the next election, Senator Steven Trahison is not only the Senate's top Republican, he is also this secret group's co-founder, rainmaker, and high priest.

He will be the one visibly leading the way after the coming purge. He's the one preparing the worthy sacrifices to be burned on the altar of renewal. While there are others in this small cabal who wield even more power than the senator, like his, their highly visible positions require that this alliance and agenda remain as silent and deep as a galaxy-swallowing black hole. Their identities known only to each other.

The crew members of the oil tanker who were already sacrificed in Wisconsin, and the few thousand more souls who are about to be, will all become heroes of the new order, not the helpless victims the liberal media will call them. I'll see to it.

Phase one is complete. Phase two underway. And perhaps even before phase three is successfully completed, H.R.7174's Presidential signature will seal and set America's new corrective course in motion.

His countenance lifted as he thought, *a liberal Democratic President signing H.R.7174 into law is my definition of poetic justice. I can see it now—President Olson, at the Resolute Desk, the bill in front of him, me standing to his right, the President hands me the first of a dozen pens he'll use to sign my bill. We shake hands. Smile for the cameras.*

At that moment, putting his feet up onto his desk and leaning his chair further back, he felt a surge of optimism. Everything was finally falling into place. Decades of planning, secret meetings, hidden communications and the moving and eliminating of strategic pieces on the chess boards of government and commerce are finally about to bear fruit. The harvest will be America's rebirth.

The America he was certain the Founding Fathers had envisioned nearly two-hundred and fifty years ago, not the diluted, dysfunctional, dystopian version that this once great nation was all too rapidly becoming.

I no longer have a choice. I must act before it's too late. I must rekindle that original vision. Reignite it with a cleansing light that will burn so bright the entire country and world will clearly see the new path at their feet, leading them all to a better future—one that I will usher in.

If only Hamilton were alive today to see it.

Chapter 10

The cacophony of voices echoing throughout the gallery's cavernous space hit Hunter with a wall of sound and a wall of people as he opened the front door. He could barely get in.

A docent squeezed through the crowd, thanked him for coming and handed him a postcard with Eve's name alongside a picture of one of her paintings. He scanned the crowd looking for Eve.

Spotting her at the far end of the space, deep in conversation with a middle-aged couple gesturing at the painting they were standing in front of, he walked over to the left wall by an office. It had a long table of plastic glasses filled with white wine and various arrangements of hors d'oeuvres and finger foods. After waiting his turn in line, he selected a glass, picked up a small paper plate from a stack, loaded a few items onto it, took a napkin and began to stroll around looking at the paintings.

The work quickly pulled him in—he became mesmerized by the many layers of deeply textured surfaces and colors. Some of the paintings bright and bold, others subdued, dark and moody. Understated imagery ran throughout the surfaces, some hinting at flowers and plants of dripping, weeping paint. Others suggesting human figures, heads, torsos and arms moving in and out the canvases. Each painting a contradiction—both elegant and raw, elusive and unflinching, graceful and menacing.

He was so absorbed that he hadn't noticed Eve standing right behind him. "Well, what do you think?" He turned to face her, his heart skipped a beat. "Oh, hi there!" The food and wine in his hands made the quick hug a bit awkward. "Honestly, I'm floored. Your work is amazing."

"You're so kind. Thank you very much!" She had been hearing similar praise all evening and was quite accustomed to be lauded, but this was the first time she felt herself blush a bit, or was it the half glass of wine?

"You're welcome. But I should be thanking you for bringing so much beauty into the world."

Yup, she felt her face get warm and a bit tingly, definitely not the wine, which both amused and surprised her.

Charlene came over. "Charlene, this is Hunter, a colleague of mine. Hunter, this is Charlene, owner of the joint."

As they shook hands, "You have an amazing gallery."

"Thank you. Quite frankly it would be nothing more than a large boring room of tall white walls if we didn't have work like Eve's to bring it to life. Her paintings make the walls breathe, don't you think?"

"Couldn't agree more." Eyes on Eve. "Stunning."

"Gee, thanks you two. Please stop or my head won't fit through the front door."

Charlene said, "Bullshit. You love it.

With an impish smile and close to a whisper, "Yes, yes, I do. I do love it."

"It was nice to meet you, Hunter. I hope you won't mind if I take our star away with me to meet a prospective buyer? I promise not to keep her too long."

"Oh, absolutely, by all means… Good luck!"

Eve said, "I'll be back." As she and Charlene turned and walked away, Charlene whispered in her ear, "You never told me you worked with George Clooney's doppelganger."

"He is cute, isn't he."

"Girl, he got me rethinkin' my sexual predilections."

But Eve didn't come right back. She kept being pulled into one conversation after another, each person or couple or small group wanting to heap praise on her for the work and ask questions. Throughout the evening Charlene continued to usher Eve by the arm to folks he assumed were collectors, or she brought them in tow over to Eve.

Hunter didn't mind. He was enjoying taking it all in. The room had a bouncy hum. He had been to a few art galleries before, but never during an opening. He could see Eve relishing the buzz. And he relished watching her. Every so often she would look his way. At first, she'd quickly look back if he noticed. But as the evening wore on, she'd offer up a small smile whenever they exchanged glances. Once she mouthed an "I'm sorry" and shrugged.

As different people came and went throughout the evening, Hunter was also approached by several women and a couple of men who struck up conversations about the art and the artist. One older guy with long, stringy gray hair and a scraggly, white, Fu Manchu mustache and beard cornered him, regaling him with his sad life's story and the woes of being an artist in this town populated with philistines who didn't buy art. At least not his art. One of the women actually asked him if he'd like to go with her for a drink. He lied, said he's married. "Too bad. Lucky woman," she said as she sauntered off. All the while, Hunter kept an eye on Eve's whereabouts.

From the moment she walked into the conference room at the police station only a few days ago, he was smitten. At first, it was for all the obvious reasons—she *is* stunning after all. But as the meeting went on, her clear intelligence, quick wit, unflappable demeanor and comfort being in command of a room drew him in even further.

His desire to spend more time with her over coffee after the meeting had more to do with simply wanting to be with her than his Bonnato questions. And he was pretty sure she could see right through his thinly veiled ruse and became even more intrigued as she played along.

He did some looking into her background after their coffee date. Reached out to a Homeland buddy who had worked with Eve and her CIA team on two domestic counterterrorism investigations. His buddy didn't tell him much more than he already got from his briefing documents before coming to Boston, with one exception—his friend was pretty sure Eve did some highly classified work in Ukraine recently.

Told him he envied Hunter for getting this gig. Said of all the folks he's worked with over the years, there were few better than Eve at counterintelligence anywhere on the planet. That in addition to acute tenacity, she had a sixth sense for it, saw connections that most missed. Proposed creative approaches that awed him and the team. Not to mention being so very easy on the eyes—what would result if Kristen Bell and Megan Fox could have had a love child.

Hunter had read her Homeland file and already knew that Eve was Canadian. Raised in Quebec by her grandparents. Specifically on the Île d›Orléans, an island located in the Saint Lawrence River, three miles east of downtown Quebec City. The French colonized this province first, and Eve's ancestor was among the original settlers of the island.

He knew Eve was one of the first women to make it into the Canadian Special Forces Command. The first and only woman so far to become part of its most elite group, Joint Task Force 2. The JTF2 team is where she saw her share of action in Afghanistan, working as part of the 3rd Special Forces Group, called Task Force K-Bar, alongside a team of Green Berets and Seals on some very high-risk, high-value ops, mostly targeting Taliban command nodes.

Everything JTF2 did was classified. No exceptions. Her performance as the planner and leader of several of these missions got the CIA's attention. The Agency's Special Activities Center (SAC), the division of the CIA responsible for covert and paramilitary operations, admired her work, approached her and she agreed to work for them. After Afghanistan, the CIA saw to it that Eve quickly gained U.S. citizenship, which was essential for her to receive the highest of the nation's five levels of security clearance: Top Secret/Sensitive Compartmented Information.

Hunter looked forward to the gallery opening all week. He couldn't believe he was actually stressing over what he'd wear, finally settling on jeans, brown leather chukka boots, white turtleneck sweater and his Navy-issued leather bomber jacket.

Shortly before ten, nearly an hour later than the opening was officially supposed to be over, the last of the chatting stragglers offered Eve their parting praise as they made their way to the door. Hunter was standing in front of the painting closest to the door, which he deemed his favorite, as Eve came over. "I'm both pumped and exhausted. I'm so glad you came, but you didn't have to stay this whole time."

"I loved every minute. It's my first opening."

"Really? Your first? I don't think I've ever been someone's first before," she said with a wink.

He said, "You hungry? Want to go someplace to celebrate this incredible night?"

"I'm too amped to eat. But I'd love a drink, something a bit stronger than wine."

"Just say where."

"I've got an unopened bottle of Pappy Van Winkle that I've been saving for a special occasion. And since every painting in here sold, I think tonight fits the bill, don't you?"

He did a mental double take. Did she just invite him to her place? "Congratulations! That's incredible! Pappy sounds great. Never had it before."

"Wow. Two firsts in one night. Give me a minute to grab my things and we can walk over. It's just two blocks. Did you bring a car?"

"No, I walked."

"Perfect!"

Eve headed over to the gallery's office. Charlene was standing behind her desk and came around as Eve entered. He watched the two of them through the glass wall—both were animatedly jubilant, laughing, hugging and jumping up and down for a few minutes.

Eve pulled her coat from the back of a chair which also held her bag, came out, walked over to Hunter while slipping on her coat. Hunter opened the door. Once out, Eve took his arm, surprising herself and him as she did, as they strolled off into the street-lit night, both completely oblivious to the cold.

Chapter 11

The blinking light on line two of his office phone told Wisconsin State Police Superintendent, Anthony Burns, that he was still on hold. Had been for nearly forty-five minutes. Just as he started eating his sandwich and was about to tell his administrative assistant, Cheryl, to try again later, she popped her head in and said, "He's on now."

As he picked up the receiver, Wisconsin's FBI Special Agent in Charge, Bill O'Brien, said, "Tony, Tony, Tony, I'm so sorry for making you wait so long. It's a madhouse here. How are things in God's country?"

"Hey, Bill. Long time no see. You know it's only a two-hour drive from Milwaukee, right? If I didn't know better, I'd think you were trying to avoid settling up our Packers bet?"

"Damn Buccaneers. So close. And, yes, I'll get up this summer. For sure."

"I'll hold you to it."

"So what's up?"

"I've got something for you. Remember the murder/robbery we had up here a few months ago, husband and wife?

"Shot and robbed in their own home?"

"Yup, the Abrams. Well, the case just took a weird twist. Neighbor kid skating on the lake by their place found one of the items stolen from their house frozen in the ice, about a hundred and fifty yards from shore. A Picasso painting."

"No...way..."

"Puts a whole new spin on what looked like a straight forward robbery and murder case. There's also a boat sittin' on the bottom below it. We cut the painting out of the ice and made a bigger hole to send a couple of divers down to take a look and retrieve anything else that might be there. That's why I'm calling."

"Whatcha find?"

"Everything the Abrams' insurance company listed as stolen was in or around the boat, which was intentionally set on fire and sunk by ten forty-caliber holes. The gun that made them was also in it. Once ballistics come back, ten will get you a hundred it's the same gun that killed the Abrams."

"Holy shit."

He kept looking at his sandwich and could no longer resist, took a bite, and between chews said, "We've retrieved everything but the boat itself. That will have to wait until spring when the ice melts and we can lift it out cleanly and not lose any potential evidence."

"Fingerprints?"

"None on the gun or any of the other stolen items. He was wearing rubber gloves. Not likely to find prints on the boat once we get it up, but we'll fine tooth it all. But here's the thing, he tossed the rubber gloves he was wearing into the boat before sinking it. One melted almost completely and one was mostly left intact. I'd like your DNA lab guys to handle it."

"I'll expedite it for sure. Apart from the lab help, what you've told me so far doesn't make this a Fed matter."

"This might. Coroner put the Abrams' death on the same night that oil tanker blew up. At the time, we made no connection between the two events. But this boat and its contents changes all that. Plus, the location of the tanker explosion is a direct line as the crow flies from the Abram's back yard. Another ten will get you another hundred that's no coincidence either, and why we're talkin' now."

"This is huge, Tony. Let's not let this out yet. Keep it quiet for the time being, if possible."

"With you there. Already spoke to the kid who found it and his folks. Asked them to not tell a soul and why. Since the Abrams' property borders a state forest preserve with nothing but wildlife as potential witnesses, as far as we know, it's still pretty contained. Spoke to each of my team. And while Door is a fairly secluded part of our state, you know how these things can go, Bill."

"I do indeed. Got some calls to make as soon as we hang up. And I promise to head your way this summer, Tony."

With a mouthful, "Your chair by the fire pit will be waiting. And I got a fresh box of cigars. Keep me in the loop, will ya."

"Will do, buddy. Talk soon."

Chapter 12

Hunter woke to the smell of brewing coffee and the bright morning sun billowing through three entire walls of floor-to-ceiling windows that he could see from the upper bedroom level of Eve's loft, overlooking the rest of the open, 20-foot-high ceilinged space.

He got out of bed, searched for his briefs among the articles of clothing strewn over the floor, put them on and headed down the open, wide oak stairs to the main floor.

He didn't get to see much of her place last night, so he was taking it all in—the walls of glass, stacks of finished paintings leaning against an inside wall next to a well-worn leather chair facing a tall, paint-crusted easel. A gray sofa and two black chairs surrounding a glass-topped coffee table in the middle of the room. A life-sized wooden sculpture of a nude woman stood in a corner. He couldn't be certain, but it looked a lot like Eve. Before they finished their first and only glass of bourbon, they were all over each other—Eve quickly leading him by the hand up the stairs he just descended.

"Hey, there," said Eve from behind the kitchen's white marble island, three tall chrome swivel chairs tucked under one side. Behind her, a stainless steel wall with a rack holding several copper pots and pans, next to a stainless fridge, stove, and oven hood, all capturing and reflecting the sunlight, made the already bright space even more so.

She wore a long, white silk robe that he noticed hugged her curves and peeked at him from all the right places. She noticed him ogling and pulled her robe more closed, a self-conscious move to cover her huge, rough scar, two inches wide, that ran all the way from her pubic bone to her sternum. A silly protective effort as she thought about it, since he clearly already knew every inch of it, as well as the rest of her body for that matter. Probably could have drawn a detailed topographical map if asked. But standing here with him now somehow felt different. She felt more exposed by the light of day and in light of cooler passions. Besides, it had only been one night. One truly amazing night, but nevertheless, her guard went back up.

"Hey there, yourself," he said walking over to her, enfolding her in his arms as she turned toward him, her coffee cup in both her hands, placing her head on his chest. They remained like this for a couple of minutes.

"I made coffee, want some?"

"Yes, please. Where are the cups?"

She pointed to the cabinets next to the fridge. "How did you sleep?"

At the cabinet. "I dreamed I was with the most beautiful woman on the planet." Animatedly gesturing toward her with both hands, doing his best wild-and-crazy Steve Martin, a wide-eyed expression and grin on his face, "And look, dreams *do* come true!"

"I think you set some sort of record for stamina. I lost count. What do they feed you over there at Homeland?"

"Oysters on the half shell for breakfast, oysters Rockefeller for lunch and smoked oysters for dinner."

"Taxpayer money well spent, I must say."

After filling his cup and placing it on the counter, "Point me to the bathroom, please."

"Through there, take a right, first door on your right."

When he returned, coffee in hand, he found her sitting on a large, L-shaped, pale gray sofa facing the center of the three walls of windows. A concrete deck with a steel-rope railing ran along the entire left glass wall, leaving the center with an uninterrupted view of downtown Boston in the distance, the John Hancock building's sun-stricken blue glass windows in the center of the clustered buildings. He sat next to her, put an arm around her shoulders and she leaned into him.

Noticing his leather jacket laying on the chair across from them, she said, "You a pilot?" On his nod, "What unit does the shoulder patch represent?" On a yellow background, a black fist held a red lightning bolt, 'VFA-25' written on a banner at the bottom.

"Strike Fighter Squadron twenty-five. The Flying Fists. Part of Carrier Wing Eleven."

"What'd you fly?"

"F/A-18 mostly."

"Ah, a Bug pilot. Sexy. So tell me, Tom Cruise, do you miss it?"

"All the time. Nothing compares to carrier cat shots strapped to a seventy-million-dollar titanium bullet. Not even sex." Grinning. "Well, perhaps until now, that is. I miss the smell of JP-8 mixed with damp, briny sea air. Even miss my green Nomex. Since we're talking insignias, tell me about the tattoo over here," as he moved her robe to access and kiss her back right shoulder.

"Canadian Special Operations Regiment." Two folded gold wings extended from an upright black dagger, surrounding all of that were two clusters of black oak leaves with two crossed gold arrows at their base, above a banner that read, 'Audeamus.'

"The word at the bottom?"

"It literally translates 'We Dare.' But, like most Latin words there's also a more poetic translation, 'May we be eager for battle.' Why'd you stop flying?"

"Vision. Left eye got worse than 20/70."

"That sucks. Spend any time in the 'Stan?"

"Yup. Once we took out the Taliban's air defense sites, airfields, and military command-and-control centers in Afghanistan, we'd fly over assigned engagement zones and provide precision firepower on-demand as ground forces needed it. When targets of opportunity were identified. You know, puttin' warheads on foreheads. Did a fair amount of time-critical targeting missions working with special forces, as you well know."

"Who knows, I may have even called you in on some of those."

"Huh… Would that count as a first date?"

"If so, then you sent me bullets instead of flowers? Not sure it will catch on with most womenfolk."

"But you're not most womenfolk."

"Thanks. But I'll still take flowers over bullets."

"I'll keep that in mind. Anyway… Ali Baba had no air force to speak of, so no dogfighting for any of us, which was disappointing. Made a lot of hops baby-sitting B52s trying to blow the Taliban out of their caves in Tora Bora. Moved plenty of mud there myself. So much, in fact, I often see that mountain topology in my dreams. Finished my tour training new jocks at the Lenmoore California base. I understand you saw a lot of action over there though."

"I did."

He saw her eyes and face go still, blank, momentarily lost in thought. Most likely a memory of one or many, or perhaps too many, of those missions, and changed the subject.

"What a view," he said.

"Isn't it amazing."

Looking directly at her, "Yeah, and the one out the window ain't bad either. I think the oysters are at it again."

"Oh my, yes, I see." Quickly placing their cups on the coffee table, Hunter nearly spilling his, they were soon entwined on the sofa.

Chapter 13

Peter went to the large horizontal freezer that took up much of the floor space in the farmhouse's mud room, right off the kitchen, reached in to retrieve a couple of steaks. He brought them into the kitchen and placed them on the island countertop to thaw.

The house had been well stocked with a wide array of food and beverages before he arrived. He only had to make an occasional trip into town for fresh eggs, fruit and half-and-half for his coffee. The powdered stuff made him gag. He also went to the local hardware store in downtown Bethlehem twice to pick up some wire, electrical tape and sheet metal rivets.

On his way in and out of town, he'd often slow down to get a better look at the life-size metal sculptures of moose made from gears, scrap metal, and old machine parts. Three of them stood in front of the Indian River Trading Company, a country store that catered mostly to tourists. They intrigued him. He thought, *If only I had the time, I think I could do something that cool. Maybe other animals, too. Perhaps someday. When this is all over and the dust settles, I could set up my own studio. Sell my stuff out front.*

To the west and south of the farmhouse, Peter had amazing views of the White Mountains. Cannon, Garfield, South Twin mountains and Mount Hale poked their snow-covered heads across most of the horizon.

Secluded enough for secrecy, but also crowded enough with large numbers of transient tourists all year round, Bethlehem was a perfect location for his work. His presence in this town of only 2,600 permanent residents was barely noticed on his occasional visits in a white Subaru with New Hampshire plates. He blended right in.

The farm's barn was set up perfectly for jury-rigging missiles. His entire list of equipment, tools and parts were all packed in their crates and boxes when he arrived. It took him a week to set everything up and get started. While he had already altered two other missiles for Lake Michigan, the four he was working on now presented different challenges to solve.

The first two must travel further than the two he had at the lake. And the initial charge that pierces the surface will need more penetrating punch. The second incendiary device that ignites after the first charge explodes will also need a bigger kick after a longer delay, only a couple of seconds. But seconds mattered. Milliseconds mattered. The final two missiles, which includes the one left over from Wisconsin, will need other tweaks, including making an allowance for cooler evening temperatures.

The Massachusetts Institute of Technology had unknowingly educated him well for this task. Peter received his degree in electrical engineering just before 9/11. And like millions of other young men and women at that time who were shocked and enraged by such a heinous attack on American soil, he joined the Armed Forces expressly to pound Al Qaeda back into the Babylonian desert sands. Like the rest of America and its allies, he was furious and highly motivated to do something about it.

The Army provided him with the remainder of the knowledge and training he'd need. Noting his M.I.T. degree and then the off-the-charts results of his vocational aptitude testing, the Army assigned him to the 10th Air & Missile Defense Command.

He became an expert in every facet of nearly every missile and defense system the Army used—the MIM-104 Patriot, the Terminal High Altitude Area Defense system, or Mad THAAD as he liked to call it, the Avenger Air Defense System, the FIM-92 Stinger, and what became his favorite and missile of choice, the FGM-148 Javelin.

For the first year of duty after boot camp, Peter served with the 5th Battalion, 4th Air Defense Artillery Regiment, learning how to operate, shoot and maintain these missile systems. But you certainly didn't need a degree from M.I.T. for that. With training, a high school diploma would suffice. And often did.

After that year in the field, Peter, now furnished with hands-on experience, began working on the missiles and launch platforms themselves, refining their operating systems, adjusting and tweaking their performance. He did this working alongside engineers from companies like

Raytheon and Lockheed Martin, the very folks who designed and built these remarkable darts of defense and death.

He discovered he really enjoyed the work and excelled at it. He felt fulfilled, believed he found his niche, perhaps his very life's purpose.

His talent was obvious and clearly noted by Raytheon, so when he finished his tour they hired him. They actually made him an extremely generous offer six months before his tour of duty ended. Peter wasted no time and started his new job a week after his discharge. And life was great for a year and a half.

Then the accident happened.

Some idiot tech working on a Stinger missile a couple of workbenches away wasn't paying attention, hadn't followed the failsafe protocols and while working on the warhead, crossed some wires that shouldn't have been live, setting off the two-and-a-half pounds of explosives designed to take down planes and helicopters—a lethally balanced mix of octogen—a high-melting explosive—TNT, and aluminum powder. It was the last mistake that tech ever made. They picked pieces of him off the walls and ceiling for a week.

Even with the protective shields set up around each workbench, Peter's proximity caused him to nearly suffer the same fate. He actually died on the operating table twice. Spent four months in an ICU, a machine breathing for him. Three more months in the hospital's post critical care ward, and then two months in a rehab hospital.

While he gradually healed physically—bones mended, internal organ swelling and functions returned to normal, muscles and ligaments repaired and rehabilitated—the damage to his brain took longer.

After the accident, he could no longer think like he used to. Easily confused and quickly agitated. More than a year later, the simple math needed to make change from a dollar challenged Peter.

Once able to do multivariable calculus equations in his sleep, eat linear algebra and probability problems for breakfast, and perform Fourier analysis and Z-transforms without breaking a sweat, he now added and subtracted using his fingers.

After three years, nearly all of what he was able to do gradually came back, but along with his mental faculties came occasional bouts of nearly blinding, incapacitating headaches that can last anywhere from many hours to mere seconds.

But, by then, the Raytheon job was long gone. The financial settlement that the company worked out with his lawyer pretty much meant he'd never need to work again. The kind of money that neither he or his parents ever thought they'd see in their lifetime.

During his junior year at M.I.T., his parents were killed in a car accident on a Pennsylvania highway one snowy winter evening as they made their way home from dinner with friends. Rounding a blind corner on a steep incline, the car slid into the opposite lane, slamming head-on into an oncoming tractor trailer, killing them both instantly. He received some life insurance money that covered their funeral and the rest of his tuition. But his parents, both teachers—dad taught high school math, mom was a beloved kindergarten teacher—didn't own or leave much else.

At the time of their deaths, their house had a mortgage that was underwater due to the timing of their purchase, when interest rates were sky high and then rapidly fell only a year later, along with the inflated value of the property, leaving them with negative equity at the time of their deaths and the bank becoming its new owner.

He thought about buying it back after the Raytheon settlement, but learning that a young family with two small children and another on the way had purchased it, he changed his mind. *Probably better off anyway. Who needs the ghosts?*

But Peter didn't simply lose a job, he lost his purpose. He became aimless, hopeless, deeply depressed and near suicidal. The depth of these feelings even surpassed what he felt after his parents died. At least then he knew his folks not only wanted him to continue on and live a full life, but at that time he also had a bright future ahead of him. What was on the horizon buoyed hope. Now that was gone, too.

Peter spent the next two years wallowing in self pity and self medication, although his alcohol and substance abuse was short lived—nearly everything he drank, swallowed, snorted, or inhaled either brought on one of his searing headaches and room-spinning dizzy spells or made them worse. He had *the* sure-fire cure for addiction, but no clinic or counselor would ever recommend it to their patients.

He was lost and adrift.

Until his uncle reached out to him and took him under his wing. Then everything changed.

Chapter 14

Eve was in her studio, standing at her easel finishing up the last strokes of white gesso with a six-inch wide brush, covering the last beige corner of the large, drum-tight canvas surface, when her cell phone rang.

It was only 8:00 a.m. on a Saturday, so she knew it wasn't Hunter, he should be flying. Figured it was probably work, or perhaps her grandmother. They were long overdue for a chat. She found herself missing both of her grandparents a lot lately.

Pulling off her paint-crusted rubber gloves, she walked to the long wood table. Four feet high and wide and on wheels, it held a rainbowed skyline of various sized jars, bottles, jugs and tubes of paint and three coffee cans filled with brushes and palette knives. She picked up her phone, recognized the number and said, "Hey, Captn,' whussup?"

"How quickly can you get here?"

"Fifteen minutes, give or take. What's goin' on?"

"FBI got a hit on the Wisconsin rubber gloves."

"Prints?"

"Just partials. But struck gold with DNA in the palm. Running it through every DNA database as we speak. We should know who this person is in two or three days. Also,

Bonnato thinks they've got something from the social media sniffer he's been running the last few months. See you when you get here." Abruptly ending the call.

Eve entered the station conference room, everyone was paired off and talking at once. "There she is," said Captain Evans, "Let's get started. Joe, tell us whatcha got." Eve and Hunter caught each other's eye, both trying hard not to smile, wanting to keep their hot and heavy four-month relationship on the down-low, especially with this group.

"Few months back I told you we were unleashing a new sophisticated algorithm targeting mostly social media."

Dick Murphy, said, "You innaccepted Sweeney's dick pics, didn chya."

Sweeney replied, "At least I got one can be seen without a micro lens, buddy."

Bonnato chuckled as he continued. "We started analyzing social traffic several days before and after the oil tanker explosion. Couple interesting things." As he handed out a sheet of paper to each. "First, some activity on Twitter caught our eye. Pinpointed one side of the conversation to Door County, near the Abram's, in fact. Phones were not on long enough for accurate cell tower triangulation. However, the first Twitter exchange that night was longer on the Wisconsin side. That's how we knew it was near or perhaps even at the Abrams place. We think he left the phone on while waiting for a reply. The other's in DC. Again, not enough time to get closer."

Murphy said, "That's no coincidence. We ID da phones?"

"No. Probably immediately turned off with batteries removed before and after use. No way to trace. Both Twitter accounts were set up with fake names and they did some pretty high-level onion routing with the IP addresses."

Murphy added, "So deah smaht."

Paper in her hand, Eve said, "It looks like he's on his way or already in northern New Hampshire. He probably drove to Chicago from Wisconsin. Flew O'Hare to Logan. Or maybe to Manchester? Unless he didn't fly commercial at all. That would open up a lot more possibilities, wouldn't it. Any more recent exchanges?"

Joe said, "Nothing yet. But now we know where to look. And they don't know we know."

Captain Evans said, "Eve, it's your call, but I think you and Joe should head to Wisconsin."

"Yup, what I'm thinking, too."

Hunter said, "We can use Homeland's Gulfstream. It's parked at Logan and ready to go. I can put us in Wisconsin in a couple hours."

Evans said, "Well, get the hell out of here then."

Chapter 15

The May breeze off Lake Michigan carried the sweetly scented promise of summer—somewhere nearby the lilacs were in bloom. Eve was standing on the Abrams' dock with Joe, Hunter, and FBI Special Agent, Jim Merchant, who picked them up from the airport in Green Bay, where he's stationed, and drove them here.

They went through the Abram's house together, walked around the long-dried blood on the floor, noted the stained beige wall and bullet hole. Did a quick run through of the kitchen and living room before heading out and walking around back to the boat dock.

To the northwest, and stretching north toward the lake and inland to the south, nothing but mile after mile of ancient beech forest—Aspen-birch, maple, basswood, spruce fir, and oak—most in various stages of budding, some with newly unfurled, tiny, pale-green leaves.

Eve said, "Jim, when you guys pulled out the boat, did you test it for any explosive residue?"

"Gasoline burns made finding anything like that impossible."

Toward the lake she said, "Is that a lighthouse on an island out there?"

"Yup, Pilot Island. About three miles from here. Small island. Three, four acres total. Old lighthouse is all that's on it. Well, that and flocks of cormorants. Built sometime in the 1850s, I think. Automated now."

"How quickly can we get a boat?"

Joe said, "What are you thinking?"

"If you wanted to use a missile to blow up a tanker, like a Stinger or a Javelin, would you want to launch it from a small outboard boat, or from something more stationary and stable, something offering an elevated shooting position, perhaps?"

"Like a lighthouse."

Jim said, "Can have a boat here in less than an hour."

Eve said, "Keys to the lighthouse, too?"

As the twenty-two foot Starcraft pulled up to Pilot Island's pier, Ron Jackson, the state trooper and boat pilot, killed the motor and jumped out to secure the bow line. Hunter hopped out and did the same with the stern, tying the line to one of the pier's crusty cleats.

After they all climbed out onto the dock, Eve said, "Look, I know it's been several months since our perp may have been here, and the chance for evidence slim, but let's keep our eyes peeled anyway, okay?"

The five of them donned their rubber gloves as they walked slowly toward the lighthouse, heads down. Joe got to the lighthouse's door first, leaned closer to the handle and keyhole lock above it and said, "These scratches. Fresh. It's been picked." He snapped a picture with his phone.

Eve came over and stood next to him with a key attached by a short chain to a two-inch round metal tag with 'Pilot Island Lighthouse" stamped on it, opened the door, walked a few steps and stopped. She said, "Footprints in the dust. Going both ways to and from the stairs and this door." She took a couple pictures.

The others followed and fanned out, headed toward the light tower's spiral stairs at the far end of the room.

Hunter was first up the steps and after taking several, said, "These dents in the plaster look pretty fresh. Kinda' deep. Something heavy perhaps?"

Eve asked, "Anyone know what a shoulder launched missile and its case might weigh?"

Joe said, "Anywhere from fifty to more than a hundred pounds. Depends on which type, and if one or two missiles are in the case."

As they continued to ascend the spiral stairs, Hunter said, "Another dent. And I can see a couple more further up. All about the same height."

They found and photographed five spots with deep dents and scrapes in the plaster. Once they got to the service room, Eve went to the door and with her cell phone's flashlight checked the knob and door edge before opening it and heading out onto the metal-railed deck. Turning around to face them she said, "Not sure this thing will hold all of us at once. Joe, come with me. Jim and Hunter, head up to the lantern room. Then head down with Trooper Jackson, take a look around the whole perimeter, then come to the side of the building where we are, will you?"

As she and Joe slowly went around the entire deck, they stopped when they were facing directly east, the vastness of Lake Michigan filling the horizon, three small islands inhabited only by trees off to the left. Pointing to the railing, Eve said, "Do these scuff marks look fresh to you?"

"Sure do."

"Some army-green colored paint flecks on the deck."

Jim, Hunter, and Jackson eventually appeared fifty feet below them. Eve called down, "Can you guys see anything on the walls around us, or anything below us seem out of place?"

Jim said, "Kinda hard to tell. It's pretty weather beat. But looks like it could be soot in one spot. Right below where you're standing."

"Jim, we have a crime scene. Get forensics out here. But we already know what they'll say."

Chapter 16

A few months earlier, Peter was in the barn working intently on a missile. And due to the roaring pair of industrial-grade space heaters he had running to ward off the February chill, he didn't hear the car pull into his driveway. Mary Brighton was Bethlehem's Welcome Wagon representative. She had been meaning to come by sooner with her basket of clear cellophane-wrapped tchotchkes bearing local business logos—coupons for free items or big savings from many of the local merchants and restaurants, a block of cheddar cheese from a local maker, a small bottle of maple syrup and a package of maple candies in the shape of maple leaves from the country store, key chains from a realtor and an insurance agent, a small flashlight, some calendars, brochures, and pamphlets.

She walked up to the farmhouse's front door and rang the bell. Waited. Rang it again. The Subaru was parked near the barn. She heard a drill whirring, so she left the porch and headed to the barn door.

She knocked, the drill whirred again. Realizing she wasn't being heard, knocking as she opened the door, slowly stepping in, "Hello? Hello, new neighbor, hope I'm not intruding. I'm Mary, Bethlehem's Welcome Wagon."

Holding the basket out in front of her, "I want to officially welcome you to our community. This is for you. It's a small token-" she gasped. Saw enough movies to recognize it. Peter had a missile clamped into a special curved vice, perfectly formed around its midsection, and he had no time to cover it.

"Is that a missile?"

"This? Sort of. I build fireworks. This one creates a very impressive, multi-level, multi-colored display."

"Oh, I've seen those." She believed him. Mostly. *I'm definitely gonna do some Googleing when I get home.*

"It's nice to meet you. Thank you so much for the gift. Very thoughtful. Let's head over the house. I'll put on some coffee, and you can tell me all about the town, okay?"

"Perfect." As she went out the door, Peter removed his Glock from the workbench drawer and slipped it into his belt at his back as he headed for the door. He took a couple of jogging strides to catch up with her.

"Is your wife home?"

"Not married. It's just me." As he came beside her, reached for the gun and shot her in the side of her head, her body dropping onto the driveway, the basket bounced a few feet, stopped near her car.

He hurried back to the barn, placed his gun on the workbench, put on a pair of rubber gloves. Returned, found her keys in her purse, picked up the basket, opened the trunk and tossed it in. He then dragged Mary's body over and did the same with her, being careful to avoid her oozing, blood-soaked head.

His nearest neighbors on either side were more than a mile away, so he wasn't worried about the gunshot raising any alarms. Besides, gunfire from what he assumed were hunters echoed off the mountains every so often at this time of year. He would be leaving in four more months, as soon as the last missile is finished and the weather turns warmer. What he needed to do now was whatever it took to buy enough time.

The farm had some woods on the north side of a long fallow field that ran east and west of the farmhouse. There was an old cow trail that ran through the middle of the woods, a shortcut the farmer used to get his herd and tractor to the hay and grazing field on the other side.

He drove her car across the frozen, snowless ground, onto the trail and about half way into the woods, turned into an opening in the trees, eased the car in as far as the space would allow, parked and got out. He came back shortly thereafter with a hatchet and hand saw and covered the car with limbs and evergreens to hide it as well as he could. The driveway was dirt and gravel, so he dug up the spot where she bled and raked some dirt and stones around until it looked like the rest.

If anyone comes to the house looking for her before it's time to depart, which I expect, my denial's plausible. I'll even let them look around. Act very concerned. Ask about her family. No one will be the wiser until they search the woods. And that probably won't happen until a couple months after I've left, perhaps even longer.

Chapter 17

The *Suez Orion* was six miles away from Boston Harbor, travelling at a speed of fifteen knots and nearing the end of its twenty-three-hundred mile journey from Trinidad.

The Coast Guard's two officers, leading a crew of ten who boarded a while ago, were finishing up their safety and threat inspection of this 930-foot long, 140-foot wide tanker, carrying forty-million gallons of liquid natural gas in its six tanks—the tops jutting above the deck like a row of giant white igloos connected to each other by a tangle of pipes and valves.

Hidden among these pipes, next to the center LNG tank, was a tracking device that one of the Coast Guard's inspection crew members just added and activated.

Petty Officer Third Class, Jason Brown, was not told the true reason for secretly placing this device. In fact, when he was summoned to the Commander's office, handed the device and instructed on how and where to activate it, he was told by doing this, and keeping it completely secret, he was serving Homeland Security—that this device would help track the ship to determine if it was aiding America's enemies by delivering LNG to off-limits ports.

Boston's Coast Guard Base Commander, Erick Shane, was passionate and persuasive as he told his Petty Officer this, because it was exactly what he was told and believed to be true. It was what the Rear Admiral initiating the order was told. And the one who told him was leveraging the military chain of command and taking advantage of its strict adherence to following orders.

The real reason for the GPS may never be discovered, or the connection to its true purpose made long after the fact.

A mile closer to the harbor, after the Coast Guard inspection crew completed their work, cleared the ship, and returned to their cutter, the Orion was met by the *Majestic*, the 53-foot pilot boat carrying Frank Martin, Boston Harbor's most seasoned Pilot.

After his boat came alongside the tanker, matching its speed, Frank stepped to the edge of the *Majestic's* bow, reached for the rope ladder that dangled from the *Orion* and clambered up the side, like a scene in a pirate movie.

Once onboard, he made his way to the ship's bridge to guide the vessel through the harbor to its final destination. Since the average depth of Boston Harbor is only twenty feet, it is vital for large ships like the *Orion* to remain in the channel that's continually dredged to maintain its fifty-foot depth.

The *Suez Orion* entered the inner harbor an hour later, reduced its speed to a crawl and was met by three tugboats to help it maneuver its way through.

Four other boats also joined the escort party—one with armed Boston Harbor Police officers, one with a Coast Guard crew manning its 7.62-millimeter, bow-mounted machine gun, another with heavily armed Massachusetts State Police officers, and the last with armed Massachusetts Environmental Police officers—all to keep every other boat at least five-hundred feet away. They'll remain on high alert for the duration of the ship's time in the harbor and when docked during the offloading phase.

Flying above and circling this scene, two State Police helicopters provided air cover. And at the end of each pier that the *Orion* passed, a parked State Police cruiser and a trooper stood by as the huge ship hugged the shoreline near Boston's North End, where the channel is deepest, lumbered past a potentially vulnerable Logan Airport, and made its way into the Mystic River's outlet, traveling a short distance up river to dock at the Datagas LNG port in Everett.

There it will berth today and tomorrow. Today it will unload its forty million gallons into a nearby field peppered with storage tanks. Tomorrow it will refuel and resupply with the food and stores its thirty-member crew will need for the return trip. The tug boats will then be the huge ship's only escorts back to the deeper outer harbor.

Chapter 18

Hunter watched Eve working on a new painting in her brightly lit studio, which takes up the entire space on the other side of the living area of her loft, this wall of floor-to-ceiling windows displayed the city's southern night skyline.

Autolux thumped through the wall-mounted speakers—as she worked, she swayed to the beat of *Sugarless* from their *Future Perfect* album. The scent of an earlier dinner's caramelized onions and sautéed scallops lingered in the air.

She dripped a clear liquid, a bit like honey, onto the canvas with a palette knife in one hand, the jar in the other. She was using her left hand for the precise work. He noticed she wrote with her left hand, but was right-handed with most tasks, and often used both hands nearly equally. Hunter asked, "Are you right handed or ambidextrous?"

"Neither, actually. I'm left handed, but I'm right-hand dominant."

"Huh. Right *and* left brained. Unusual."

"It's called cross dominance. Or mixed handedness. Just makes me a double threat," she said with a wide smile that melted him on contact.

She moved her arm in long spiral arcs as the liquid dripped across the surface of the canvas that was lying flat on the floor when her phone rang.

She stopped, put the jar and knife down, removed her rubber gloves as she went over to the futon where Hunter sat with a glass of bourbon, bent over to give him a quick kiss and said, "It's late. Wonder who it is." She picked up the stereo's remote to quiet the music then grabbed her phone, "It's Evans…. Hey, Captn', what's up?"

"Sorry for the late hour. Two things. First, the residue on the lighthouse matches fuel used by shoulder launched missiles. Could be Stinger or Javelin. Both use it. But here's the real kicker; just got DNA results from the Wisconsin rubber glove. You're not going to believe who our murdering terrorist is." Not waiting for a reply, "His name is John Trahison."

"Wait. Trahison. As in Senator Trahison?"

"Yup. His nephew. Meeting's here at seven sharp tomorrow. Bring Hunter with you."

"Wha… he's… I'm…"

"I've known about you two for a while. Don't worry. My lips are sealed. See you first thing." And hung up.

Eve stared blankly at her phone, like it was some foreign object she'd never seen before as Hunter asked, "What was all that?"

"Senator Trahison's nephew is our terrorist. Lighthouse tested positive for rocket fuel. And the captain knows about us."

"Holy shit. Trahison's nephew? Could the senator be the DC phone? Damn... What a head spin that is. You were right about the missile. No surprise. And I had a feeling the captain was on to us. But who cares? We're not compromising anything. We're only talking optics here, really."

"I know, but for the sake of team cohesion-- doesn't matter, said he'd keep it to himself anyway. We can't jump to conclusions about the senator. He may be clueless. But if he is part of this, that's huge. He's also the minority leader. And that's titanic. Gonna' be difficult to sleep tonight."

With a smirk, arching his eyebrows up and down, Hunter said, "I have an idea for what we can do instead."

Chapter 19

Peter, aka John, drove the Subaru south on Route 93, over the Zakim Bridge and into the central artery tunnel, travelling under the city's heart. The familiar route triggered memories of the eight years he lived in this city that became his adopted home.

He loved Boston year round, but especially late spring, early summer. As a freshman at M.I.T., he did all of the typical touristy things: walked the Freedom trail, visited the USS Constitution, the old Statehouse and site of the Boston Massacre, the Boston Tea Party Ship and Museum, Bunker Hill, the Granary Burial Ground, where the remains of Samuel Adams, John Hancock, Benjamin Franklin's parents and many others rest. He also attended a few Red Sox games at Fenway. Took a duck boat tour of the Charles River and inner harbor. And all year long, John spent countless hours geeking out at the Museum of Science, even becoming a member.

John fluently assimilated into the city's seasonal rhythms. He sat out on his stoop on warm summer evenings drinking cold beer. Discussed the Red Sox pitching bench during spring training. Went apple picking in Concord in the fall, and in the winter put a folding chair in the street to mark and claim the parking spot he had shoveled out of the snow. While he was from Pittsburgh, Boston was his true home.

He pushed these memories aside and hardened himself for the task at hand.

Twenty-five minutes after entering the tunnel, he pulled into the parking lot at the Freeman Yacht Club in Quincy, turned into a secluded, not so-well-lit section of the lot near the west-side fence and parked.

He opened a small FedEx package that arrived at the farmhouse yesterday, spilled its contents onto the seat—a set of keys and a plastic key card. He put the key card into his shirt pocket, the set of keys went into his pants pocket. He then removed his Glock from under the seat, silencer added before he left the farm, got out and slipped the gun into his belt at his back. A waft of the ocean's tangy, briny breath made him pause, close his eyes and inhale deeply before walking to the marina's main gate.

It was near midnight and the marina was closed to visitors, accessible only to members with berthed boats. Peter pulled the key card from his shirt pocket, held it to the gate's lock, a faint beep, tiny green light, a click and the gate opened. He went through and stood still as the gate clicked closed behind him.

He then headed down a ramp to the wide main dock, light poles on every-other pier post illuminating the way. Continued past the closed and dark two-story, weather-beaten gray-shingled yacht club building, a red double-door at the top of six wooden stairs, past a row of three gasoline pumps, to the last row of piers that connected to the main dock like teeth on a zipper.

He turned right, past a dozen gently bobbing boats, mostly cabin cruisers, a few sailing schooners peppered in, one or two quite long and resplendently dressed in highly polished teak, masts with pristine sails expertly furled and bundled.

There was a light spilling from the cabin windows of one of the boats at the other end of main dock, one of a number of owners who sometimes choose to make their boat a weekend getaway lodge, but never actually leave the dock. *I wonder if some live here year round? I can definitely see the appeal. Who wouldn't want to be gently rocked to sleep by the ocean every night?*

He stopped in front a new Bertram Flybridge. No name on the stern, and noting the registration numbers on the bow, he stepped aboard. The thirty-five-foot long cabin cruiser was set up for sport fishing, poles stuck in their holders on each of the stern gunnel corners. A chair that he thought belonged in a barber shop was attached to the middle of the main deck—a large-reeled, long, thick fishing pole jutted from a holder by the chair's right armrest. A second empty holder in the middle of the seat, right by the crotch. *Must be for big game fish. Perhaps tuna or swordfish. Maybe stripped bass?*

Peter had never fished in his life, but his cover in Wisconsin and this setup on the Bertram both provided fitting camouflage. His father would have likely made a dad-joke about something or other being fishy, spouting a rather on-the-nose pun—the bad pun being the very essence of most dad-jokes.

He hadn't thought about his dad in quite some time. He began to wonder what his father would think about all that he and his dad's brother were up to? He knew his father and uncle were always close, only two years apart in age, and remained so right up to the day of the fatal crash. The thought of the crash made him snap back to the task at hand.

He stepped to the back of the stern. A black, fourteen-foot inflatable rubber skiff with an outboard motor was secured to the Bertram's gunnel cleat. It bobbed in the protected marina's gentle waves.

With one of the keys from his pocket, he opened the door to the main cabin and walked in, found and flipped a light switch—lots of polished reddish-brown teak wood against bright, white walls and cushions, a full bathroom with shower to the right. Further in toward the bow, through another door was the stateroom; the bed taking up most of the space. A countertop and stove were directly to his left, a small fridge next to it. Everything fit together like Tetris blocks, each square inch serving form and function with a touch of opulence.

He switched off the light. Back out to the main deck, he climbed one of two chrome step ladders that hung on each side of the boat leading up to the flying bridge. After slipping the other key into the ignition, he climbed back down, hopped onto the dock and headed back to the parking lot.

He slid out one of the two missile cases from the Subaru's cargo hold and carefully put it down. He had painted both missile cases white and added stickers of several sport fishing equipment logos. Using both hands and leaning opposite its weight, he walked the missile back to the boat and stowed it in the stateroom. He repeated the process with the second case, all the while his head on a swivel as he made his way back and forth from boat to parking lot.

On his third trip he retrieved a cooler holding the food and water he'd need for the next week and his backpack containing some clothes, a first-aide kit, a hunting knife, shaving kit, a smart watch, two boxes of ammunition and an extra magazine for his Glock, and a loaded Beretta Tomcat.

He placed the pack and cooler beside the car, reached into the glove box to retrieve a package of Clorox disposable wipes and wiped down everything he may have touched in the car's interior, the back cargo area, and the door handles.

He put the backpack on, picked up the cooler and tossed the wipes into a trash can next to the front gate as he walked by. When he got to the boat, he stowed the cooler, untied the bow and stern lines and with a shove off the dock with his foot, jumped in.

He made his way up to the bridge and placed his backpack on the floor by his feet. As he sat on the white-leather cushioned chair, he bounced a couple of times noting its supple softness. He brought the twin engines to throaty life, hit the toggles for the running lights, pushed the throttle slightly and slowly made his way to the end of the docks.

He switched on the boat's navigation screen next to the steering wheel, the screen immediately glowed in dark mode, noting his current location. He slid his finger across the screen, marked his destination and the app automatically plotted the course he should follow, keeping to the correct sides of the buoys marking the deepest and safest channels in the harbor.

He took the smart watch out of his backpack, strapped it on, scrolled through a few apps and opened the GPS—a blinking red light moved slowly to his north. With his normal cell phone he sent a quick text. Holding his second burner phone, he inserted the battery, opened Twitter and typed before removing the battery and dropping the phone back into his pack. He then scrolled to Twitter on his normal cell, saw the Tweet and said, "Excellent." He then shut the phone off and tossed it overboard, hitting the water with a plop.

Once he cleared the marina's breaker wall, he pushed the throttle further, gaining speed as he headed north-by-northeast into the moonless night, lights from the city winked on his left, inky ocean blackness to his right.

Chapter 20

Senator Trahison stepped out of the elevator and headed down the hallway toward his office when his phone made a text-message ping from his inside suit-coat pocket. Noted who it was from as went through the reception area and was greeted by his assistant. "Good evening, Senator." Picking up his pace, making a bee-line for his office, he said, "Good evening, Grace, please see that I'm not disturbed for the next half hour. Hold my coffee 'til then, too, please."

"Certainly, Senator. Everything okay?"

He didn't answer her as he closed the door behind him, dropped his briefcase onto his desk chair, pulled out the phone that not even Grace knew he had, added the battery, opened Twitter to read, "Goose flew south, ready to lay eggs. In five minutes it can no longer squawk." The Senator posted, "Boston's forecast calls for heavy rain."

He removed the battery and dropped it and the phone into his briefcase. He went to one of his office windows. The evening commute was thick—bumper-to-bumper taillights, pumping like red platelets through arteries, perfectly timed with the steady beat of the traffic lights. A hive of humanity traversed Delaware Avenue's street-lit sidewalks.

He began chewing his fingernails, a lifelong habit he had finally broken and stopped doing many years ago. In the distance he stared blankly at the flood-lighted fountain in the middle of Upper Senate Park, his mind raced as he looked at everything but noticed nothing.

Chapter 21

Eve and Hunter arrived early and were already sitting at opposite ends of the conference table with their coffees, Eve's MacBook open in front of her, Hunter held his tablet, scrolling with his finger as everyone else filtered into the room a few minutes later.

Captain Evans was standing, quickly shifting his weight from foot to foot, drumming on the table with a pencil as he waited for everyone to grab coffee and settle. As he walked around the table handing everyone a few stapled sheets of paper, he said, "Alright, boys and girls, here's what we know and don't know. John Trahison. His life's highlights on these sheets. No need to repeat it all. What we don't know is the alias he's using. Joe, what's the FBI got so far?"

Bonnato picked up a remote control and turned on the large flat-screen monitor mounted to the the wall above the coffee credenza. A few clicks brought up Trahison's Army headshot next to his bio. "Before we get to that, I want to show you all something I just received from the Bureau early this morning. It's not in the paperwork you've got there."

Clicking the remote, a report came onto the screen, he continued, "This is a psych evaluation that was done sometime after his accident at Raytheon, and then again in a follow-up exam a couple years later. Normally this is protected medical info that we wouldn't have, but score one for the Patriot Act.

"I'll sum up. Trahison's traumatic brain injury has essentially turned him into a poster child for psychopathy. While it took a few years for him to regain most of his pre-injury cognitive abilities, he broke the gauge when they evaluated and measured his psychological condition. There's a twenty-item Hare Psychopathy Checklist that shrinks use to measure this and our boy here scored a thirty-nine."

Murphy asked, "Meanin' what, exactly?"

"Trahison's score is the same as Ted Bundy's."

"Holy shit," Sweeney said.

Murphy replied, "*Unholy* shit, ya mean."

Joe continued. "This is what we're dealing with. Trahison's an extremely intelligent, remorseless, trained killer who knows nearly every U.S. missile inside and out. The Bureau also discovered that he received additional Special Forces' training, augmenting what he got at Army basic.

Sweeney said, "Remorseless doesn't even come close. Who the hell kills two people in their own home, then strolls into their kitchen to make something to eat?"

"So here's what we're doing to find him." Clicking to change images, "We're reviewing footage from Logan arrivals starting around the date of the Twitter exchange several months ago. Facial recognition app's started running as soon as we confirmed Trahison's ID yesterday. We've also got every traffic cam throughout New England downloading data from the last twelve months, running facial scans. These are on two tracks, real time and then from most recent into the past, starting here in Boston and then working outward."

Sweeney asked, "Why backwards?"

"We think he may be in Boston now, or on his way. If he's planning to hit an LNG tanker, there's one heading into the harbor as we speak. Won't be another arriving until the fall."

Murphy said, "How much time we got?"

Eve answered, "Providing he doesn't hit the ship on its route into the harbor, once the tanker docks, it's only there for one or two days, tops. That first day is extremely critical. It unloads all of its cargo in the first twelve hours. It's most vulnerable then."

Going to the map, pointing with his pencil, Captain Evans said, "The tanker's in the inner harbor now. I alerted State police and Coast Guard last night. With the Coast Guard base right here in the North End, they're pushing out everything that floats."

Joining Evans at the map, Eve said, "We need to pay attention to the lighthouses. Especially these two, Long Island and Deer Island."

Circling it with his pencil, Captain Evans said, "Deer Island was rebuilt several years ago. 2016, I think. The original concrete and brick foundation's still there, but they built a steel lighthouse structure next to it. It's nothing more than exposed steel girders. Completely wide open. Light on top. No place to hide. Anyone on it would be seen from miles away. Not ruling it out, but it's easy to keep an eye on."

Murphy asked, "Ahn't they both too fah away? Range on a Javelin's what, three miles max? How fah for da Stingah?"

Eve answered, "About five miles."

"So he'll need to get closah."

"Perhaps. He did hit the tanker on Lake Michigan from five miles out."

"So, a Stingah then."

"Maybe. Stingers are designed mainly for taking out aircraft. Some ground targets. But as designed, it lacks the kind of punch it took to obliterate the double-hulled oil tanker. Javelin's built for tanks. He may have altered it somehow. Remember, he not only operated all of the Army's missiles, he helped the designers and manufacturers tweak their performance."

Hunter said, "Could be why he came east months ago. Needed time to work on them. If we can locate where he's been, we'd know for sure."

Joe said, "We'll find out soon enough."

Murphy said, "Both a dose lighthouses ah more dan seven miles away, maybe eight."

Hunter said, "And aren't both missiles point, track and shoot? The ship would need to be physically visible in the target display, at least until it's fired. Look where the tanker docks. Well hidden from the harbor. All these buildings in the sightline. I think we need to rethink the lighthouse idea and look at other likely places to shoot from. Nearby buildings. Bridges. He could even shoot from his boat."

Sweeney said, "Shit. The Tobin Bridge. It's a clear, straight shot."

Evans added, "I think Hunter's onto something. I'm less worried about lighthouses than I was a few minutes ago."

Eve said, "I hope you're both right."

"Me, too. Got a meeting with the mayor and governor in an hour. I think they'll want to mobilize the National Guard for the next two days. While we can't be everywhere, perhaps visible manpower will be a deterrent."

Bonnato said, "More likely he'll see it as just another challenge to rise to."

Captain Evans spoke. "Look, this is fast-moving and critical. Call your wives and/or significant others and let them know you won't be home tonight, just don't tell them why. We're gonna to stay right here working this thing until the tanker is on its way back to bumfuck Egypt or wherever else it's heading next. We can take turns and catch naps on my office couch."

Murphy said, "Hey, Sweeney, bumfuck Egypt is wheah youah from aint it?"

"No, but it's where I meet your wife twice a week."

Chapter 22

John Trahison opened his eyes to the rising sun's finger poke. Warm, dust-infused beams punched through two east-facing windows of the service room in the Long Island lighthouse.

But it was a helicopter's thumping blades that actually woke him five minutes before his smart watch alarm was set to go off.

The helicopter was circling and getting closer, a pressing wall of sound in his chest. John climbed the eight metal stairs spiraling to the lantern room, slowly lifted the hatch door a crack. The Massachusetts State Police logo wagged on the helicopter's tail, one of the side doors was open, a trooper sat with his feet over the edge resting on the landing skid, a telescoped rifle on his lap. The copter made a second tight turn around the lighthouse before it rose and headed north.

His heart now raced as he made it down to the service room, took the gun from his back belt, placed it next to him and sat by the missile case. He removed a full ammo magazine and a bottle of water from his backpack, tucked the magazine into his pocket, opened the water and took a long drink.

His smart watch's tracking app indicated he had another hour, the red dot was still moving slowly, now well into the Mystic River, directly under the Tobin Bridge, nearly at the LNG port's dock.

He closed his eyes, hoping to at least rest. He'd only slept for two hours.

It had been a busy night.

After leaving the marina, he had headed north by northeast, keeping Thompson Island on his right. He was actually surprised by how many other boats were out on the harbor that late at night. Since it was mid June and quite warm, perhaps it was not that unusual.

After clearing Thompson in a mile and a half, he turned southeast, keeping Spectacle Island on his left. Another mile brought him to the southwestern tip of Long Island, sitting in the harbor shaped like a foot in a stocking.

He then headed north by northeast again, and just as he passed Rainsford Island, with only another half mile to go to reach his destination, a Boston Police Harbor Patrol boat came up on his starboard side hard and fast, bubble-gum lights flashing, a blinding searchlight beam moved across his boat and hit him in the face.

A megaphoned voice said, "Cut your engines, hold steady and prepare to be boarded. Let's see your hands."

He nearly panicked and for a half a second, thought about making a run for it, then calmed himself and obliged.

As the patrol boat pulled up beside him, two officers tossed rubber bumpers over the side of their boat to cushion the union. Two others armed with automatic weapons stood on the deck behind a metal railing that ran the length of the police boat, one stood on the bow, the other closer to the stern.

"What's going on? What's this about?"

As two officers stepped into John's boat, guns out, one quickly tied the boats together. As they bobbed in unison on the rolling ocean, the other officer said, "Routine check, sir. Are you alone?"

"Yes."

"Mind if we check?"

"Help yourself. Should I come down?"

"No. Stay where you are, please. And keep your hands where we can see them." The two officers standing on the police boat were joined by the third officer who was piloting it. He had his Glock cupped in both hands as he stood on the deck near the pilot house.

John could hear the officers open the cabin door, go in, and a minute later one called, "clear." He could hear them opening and closing cabinets and rustling about. His backpack was on the floor in front of him under the steering console and he nudged it further in with his foot, making the black pack nearly invisible in the well's shadow. He hoped.

The two officers then came out from the cabin and John breathed a bit easier. They obviously didn't find the missile cases hidden under the bed beneath a secret panel. The officers proceeded to look in the enclosed storage areas under the gunnels along both sides and stern of the main deck. One came up the ladder and nosed around the bridge. John's heart raced. "Can I see some ID, please." John reached into his back pocket for his wallet, removed his New Hampshire driver's license and handed it to him.

"Heading out to fish, Mr. Holt?"

"Yup. Hear the Bluefins are running several miles out. Somewhere around Thieves Ledge."

"Alone?"

"Absolutely. Nothing clears my head like being out here by myself."

"What do you do for a living, Mr. Holt?"

"I'm an electrical engineer."

"Stressful?"

"Can be."

To the other officers, "Okay, boys, we're good to go."

To John, "Sorry for the inconvenience, sir. Good luck. Hope they're biting."

John was nearly giddy when the officer climbed back down to the main deck. The other officer was already back on the police boat, holding onto John's boat until his partner climbed back on and then pushed the two boats apart. It throttled up and headed south, a widening white, rooster-tail wake lit by its running lights. Two bouncing red and blue lights receded into the darkness, turned left then disappeared behind Rainsford Island.

With his still-shaking hand, he started the boat, checked his heading as the screen lit up and then pushed the throttle forward. He started whistling Darth Vader's Imperial March.

Twenty minutes later, at the southwestern tip of Gallops Island, he rounded a massive stone breaker wall. The running lights illuminated a large T-shaped wooden dock poking out fifty-feet from the rocky shore. It was completely empty, as expected. The entire island was deserted. Closed to the public a few years ago when asbestos was discovered in the buildings that the military built and used seventy-five years ago.

Like most of the thirty-four islands that peppered Boston Harbor, Gallops had a long and rich military history. During the Civil War, it housed three thousand Union soldiers. At the height of WWI, the island held an infirmary for the thousands of American soldiers who contracted the Spanish Flu and pneumonia, a steady stream of sick soldiers replacing the dead.

During World War II, it hosted two military schools, one for cooks and bakers, the other for radio handlers. Today, the only permanent inhabitants occupying its twenty-three acres of grassy, shrub-covered bluffs and rocky shores were rabbits. Lots of rabbits.

John killed the running lights as he neared the dock, eased the boat parallel to it, bumped it a bit harder than he wanted as he nosed it in and hoped out, securing the boat lines to the dock's cleats.

All told, the eight and a half mile trip took nearly four hours. *Could have reduced the time by more than half by taking the more direct route the GPS initially laid out, turning South after Long Island. But thought I'd avoid the amplifying*

*number of police and Coast Guard craft in the main channel.
So many more than I thought would be out here.*

He knew police and Coast Guard vessels escorted LNG
tankers into the harbor, a practice started after 9/11, but
these were all over the place. Perhaps protocols changed.
Or perhaps they got a whiff of what he was up to. That
thought caused him to play it a bit more cautious, not from
fear for himself, but for the mission. So he took the longer,
less trafficked way around the islands.

"Fat lot of good that did." *With the LNG tanker now
making the last leg of its trip, soon docking in Everett, most of
the protective flotilla should go west with it.*

He went to the stern, pulled the rope attached to the
rubber outboard skiff he'd been towing and tied it right next
to the Bertram. He then put on a black hooded sweatshirt,
matching his black sweatpants and sneakers and added a
black baseball cap with a Chicago Blackhawks logo he'd
picked up at O'Hare.

He then retrieved one of the missile cases and gingerly
placed it into the skiff, then his backpack.

Before climbing into the bobbing rubber outboard,
he locked the cruiser's cabin door, although he wasn't very
worried about a break in. Not even the police found his
hidden missiles.

He climbed into the skiff, gave the rubber ball attached
to the gas tank a couple of squeezes, pulled the outboard
motor's cord twice before it burbled to life. He untied it
from the cruiser, retrieved a headlamp from his backpack,
turned his baseball cap backwards, stretched the rubber

strap onto his head and switched the light on. He then tucked his Glock into his belt at his back. Grasping the tiller, he twisted the throttle, the skiff swiftly headed south.

Once past the breaker wall, he pointed the boat northwest, heading for the top portion of Long Island, on its southeastern side, a little more than half a mile away across the Nubble Channel. He turned the throttle as far as it could go, sending the skiff bounding and bouncing across the water. *I won't be as lucky if the police stop me this time, that's for sure.*

Fifteen minutes later, he tugged the boat onto the island's rocky shore, carefully dragged it twenty feet across the rocks and a few feet into the tree line. He lifted the missile case out, opened his backpack, took out a hunting knife with a serrated edge on the back of the blade and proceeded to cut several evergreen and oak branches from nearby trees to camouflage the skiff.

The lighthouse was on the opposite side of the island from where he entered, its automated, battery-powered beam swept overhead, slicing through the blackness and treetops, a very bright but impotent Star Wars lightsaber.

Driving the skiff around to the northwest corner would have given him much easier and quicker access to the lighthouse, but it would have also exposed him to the open harbor. His earlier experience with the police nixed that idea.

Entering from this side of the island meant walking approximately six hundred feet into a heavily wooded area carrying more than a hundred pounds. He knew the trees would provide some cover, which could be more important for his return trip in the daylight. He figured that since he would be walking past Fort Strong, there would be some roads or at least some well-trod trails around the old fort and gun battery. Built in 1899 and, up until 1920, its 10-inch cannons protected the harbor. With the last of its guns removed in the early 40's, during WWII the fort served as an Army Intelligence post.

Fort Strong stretched from east to west across most of the distance he needed to walk. Along the way, he stopped several times to put the case down and rest, listen and look around.

He sighed with relief at the paved road that led toward the lighthouse. Although it was heavily encroached on all sides by wild vines, thick undergrowth and shrubs. Some hearty plants poked right through the middle of the pavement to bloom. He thought, *Nature is, if anything, powerfully persistent.*

The beam on his forehead lit up the fort's cracked and crumbling moss and lichen-covered concrete walls. Further down the road he came across a row of five long-abandoned huts entwined with stands of sumac and poplar trees.

Twenty minutes later, at the edge of the clearing where the lighthouse was located, he stopped, turned off his head lamp and waited a few minutes, listening intently, hand at his back on his gun. He then walked quickly across the grassy clearing, illuminated by the lighthouse twenty five feet away.

Attached to the white cylindrical lighthouse was a small square building that jutted out at the base of the phallic structure like a square scrotum, one window on each side, a red-shingled roof and green wooden door. At the top, the sweeping light illuminated the black lamp house roof, its deck and railing, tall glass panels and door. The only evidence of the house where the light keeper and his family once lived more than a hundred years ago was the outline of its stone foundation that poked up from the grass and weeds ten feet away.

He picked the door's lock, went up the winding stairs to the service room, just below the lantern room, which capped the fifty two foot tall brick tower. Unlike Pilot Island, this lighthouse had no railed observation deck at the service room level, just ten narrow, arched windows evenly spaced around the cylindered walls to observe boat traffic and weather conditions while remaining protected.

The only deck on this lighthouse was at the very top, surrounding the lantern room. He'll be completely exposed. The lighthouse was on a bluff, the trees cleared back twenty five feet all the way around it. But he won't be out in the open for long.

Chapter 23

Eve poured another cup of coffee, took one of the breakfast burritos from the McDonalds bag someone brought in and sat down. As she unwrapped her sandwich, Joe Bonnato burst into the room, "Gather 'round boys and girls, this is hot!"

He picked up the remote, after a few clicks an image from a traffic camera came up. "Just got these." He zoomed on a white Subaru Outback, then closer on the driver. "Here's our boy. Taken on the Zakim Bridge last night around eleven thirty. He's grown a beard, but no doubt it's him. Clicking again. "And these images are from Logan several months ago. Seems John Trahison has been using the name Peter Holt.

"We backtracked the car's plates to the day and time of his flight and got him from Logan, heading North on Route 93 as you see here. Tracked him all the way up through tolls to Franconia and then nothing else on 93. We think he got off here at the Route 142 exit and made his way to Bethlehem."

Eve asked, "How do we know he ended up in Bethlehem?"

"On a hunch, I searched police reports for the region. Several months ago, a missing person report was filed by the husband of Mary Brighton, fifty-five year's old, Bethlehem's Welcome Wagon lady. She was supposed to deliver a package to...wait for it... Peter Holt, who had recently moved into a farm located on the northern edge of town.

Eve whispered, "Shit."

"She went missing that day. Local police went to Trahison's house the following day and he claimed he never saw her. Cops went back two more times. He even let them look around. They found nothing.

"I called the FBI's New Hampshire satellite office in Bedford and told all of this to Agent Jason Baxter, who went with a team of agents and some state and local officers. They all got there a couple hours ago. Just sent me these." Joe clicked the remote again bringing up images of a house and barn, then images from inside the barn.

Sweeney said, "Holy shit. That vise. It's built to hold a missile. And everything looks brand new."

"Baxter called in the forensics team and they'll soon go through the entire place. Couple troopers drove around the property and, in the middle of some woods on the farm, they found Mary Brighton's car, her decaying body in the trunk, nine-millimeter hole in her head."

Eve said, "Must have seen something she shouldn't have."

Hunter said, "So where's Trahison now?"

"Traffic cams tracked him into and through the O'Neill tunnel, out onto the surface expressway and then lost him somewhere in Quincy. Doesn't look like he went any further, at least not on the expressway. Side roads pose a bigger tracking problem. Number of cameras and locations varies from town to town. It'll take longer to go through them. Algorithm's on it now."

Murphy went to the map with a burrito still in its wrapper and pointed with it, "Quincy, huh. Right on the watah. Got several marinahs. Couple here in Nort Quincy. Tree more heah to da south, ana couple more furdah down." As he headed for the door, he unwrapped his sandwich, took a bite and between chews said, "I'll call Quincy PD right now to check 'em all out ASAP. Bet one of 'em's gowt owah Subaru. Wit any luck, Trahison's still theah."

Evans said, "Let's send an APB out with Trahison's alias and photo. Make sure everyone on land and water gets it. Flag him armed and extremely dangerous. Be nice to get him alive, but no one should hesitate to drop him."

Eve said, "We can't put out an All Points Bulletin. Not yet. If the senator is involved, it will tip him off. He may even be leading this thing. If so, we need to know. Can we limit the APB to Harbor Patrol? We can easily open it up statewide and nationally later if we need to. If Trahison's got a boat, where's he headed? He could certainly shoot a missile from it. Does this put the lighthouses back in play?

Evans said, "I'll want confirmation that he's on the water before I limit the APB to Harbor Patrol. We can hold off a couple hours. That's it. Senator or no senator, the safety of our citizens comes first."

Eve said, "Understood. And agree.

Sweeney added, "Now that we have his alias, let's track his phone."

Evans said, "Already on it."

At the map, Joe said, "If he's got a five-mile range, he could go anywhere in here, middle and lower harbor. Makes sense to keep the heavy patrols going for the entire two days the tanker's here, especially within this five-mile radius. We should add more air cover, too. Captn', are the choppers armed?"

"State birds, no. They're not gunships. But we could put a shooter in them. Since the Governor called up the Guard, I'll reach out to see what they've got and if they can help. State police also have SWAT teams, so we should be covered."

Eve said, "I already know there are two Kiowa Warrior helicopters at Hanscom Air Force Base. I'll call. We should be able to get at least one of them."

Joe added, "Great. And to cover Eve's concerns, have the State birds buzz the lighthouses regularly."

Eve said, "Let's make certain Hanscom and Logan traffic towers are constantly talking. Hunter can you make that call?"

"Absolutely."

Murphy burst into the room. "Got 'em on the furst try! Quincy officahs found Trahison's Subaru in the pahkin' lot at the Freeman Yaht Club. But he's not theah." Walking over to the map and pointing, "It's right heah. Detectives and forensics are headin' theah now."

Hunter asked, "Any surveillance cameras?"

"Doh know yet. Quincy guys ah trackin' down the managah and that'll be one of theah first questions. If dey do, we'll get da footage. We should also be able to fine out wha kinna boat he's got."

Captain Evans said, "Okay. That's confirmation. The APB can go to Harbor Patrols only. For now. If the fucker's out there, we should spot him."

Eve added, "Hopefully in time."

Sweeney said, "Amen to that."

Chapter 24

In an attempt to calm himself for the hour he'd need to wait, John thought of one of the last times he and his uncle got together at the lake house, two years ago in July.

The senator's summer home is in upper-state New York. On the northern tip of Cayuga Lake, one of the idyllic Finger Lakes carved so beautifully into the landscape by a glacier hundreds of millions of years ago.

This was no small cabin in the woods, but a spacious, three-thousand square-foot, west-facing, open-floor-plan house, set back one hundred feet from the water's edge. A deeply forested national wildlife refuge on the distant eastern shore, the Catskill Mountains covered much of the northern horizon.

The entire front of the stained redwood building, from the ground floor to the tip of it's forty-foot-high peak, a wall of windows looked out through the trees, the perfect view to watch the setting sun paint a new masterpiece at the end of each day. *If there is a heaven*, John thought, *this is definitely what it will look and feel like.*

He had fond memories of this place dating back to early childhood, when his parents would drive up from Pennsylvania every summer to spend two weeks with his aunt, uncle and cousin, who was the same age as John. They were born the same year, John just four months older.

After his cousin, Richard, died of cancer at age 15, Uncle Steve and Aunt Sarah stayed at the lake house for an entire year. He was not yet a senator and the law firm where he was a senior partner gave him as much time off as he needed and wanted. John guessed that was part of the reason why his uncle sought to spend so much time with him. He was in some way a surrogate for Rick.

But he also knew his uncle loved him in his own right and was quite proud of him. Had been his entire life. As he got older, Uncle Steve loved telling people that his nephew was at M.I.T. And when he worked at Raytheon, he'd regale anyone within earshot that his nephew was an M.I.T-educated rocket scientist.

After John's parents were killed, Uncle Steve called him often just to chat, invited him to Washington to stay with them and let him know he was free to stay at the lake house anytime he wished. Even sent him his own key.

After his Raytheon accident, his aunt and uncle visited him at the hospital several times. While they kept up a hopeful and encouraging facade, the look in their eyes relayed their deep worry. He was just now realizing how difficult it must have been for them to visit. It must have brought back so many cruel and unwelcomed memories of the countless hospital visits they made for more than two years as cancer hollowed out their only child before their eyes.

Once his uncle became a senator and then, several years later, his party's leader in the Senate, visits and calls became less frequent. While he understood why, it still stung a bit, and served to deepen his depression after the missile accident. So when his uncle called him three years ago and they started meeting and talking more regularly, John felt a missing piece of himself return.

He'd do anything for his uncle. So when the senator began to lay out his plan that night, as they drank bourbon and smoked cigars on the lake house deck—dense stars of the Milky Way splattered like white paint across a black canvas, a pair of barred owls calling to each other punctured the silence, the smell of wood smoke from the fire pit wafted and mingled with the cigars—it took very little convincing for John to be all in.

He had no feelings one way or the other about so many people being sacrificed, nor did the realization that their deaths would be at his own hand effect him. He saw the bigger picture clearly. The price seemed reasonable. Unavoidable, actually.

After sipping his drink, his uncle said, "You do know that I'll need to disavow you if you get caught or they discover who you really are."

"I understand. Makes sense."

"Could get quite ugly. Hard to hear. I'll need to separate myself from you vehemently in every possible way." As he leaned closer, "But listen to me, John, it's important that you know it will all only be a front, a facade. Behind the scenes I'll do everything else within my power, and then some, everything I can to help you."

Relighting his cigar with the torch lighter, John said, "I know you will. But I won't get caught."

"Of course not. You're too smart. And there are folks pulling other connecting strings in the background and in the margins. But shit can go sideways. If there's anything I've learned in life and in my years serving in the Senate it's that shit happens. And it usually quickly goes sideways. You were trained as an engineer, so you know the importance of planning for unintended consequences. We'll need to do as much of that as possible."

"You bet. One of my strengths."

"Good. So, next steps. I've arranged for some additional training for you. Three months with a private security firm run by some trusted former Special Forces folks."

"You know I served in the Army, Uncle Steve."

As the senator filled his glass from the bottle on the small teakwood table between them, he said, "This is for stuff you didn't get in basic. More lethal hand-to-hand. Weapons training. Boat operations. Navy Seal-type shit. Stuff you'll need. I won't send you out there unless you're completely prepared, understand?"

"Got it."

"We'll also need a secret way to communicate. Any ideas? What if we use that encrypted messaging app I heard so much about, Signal... right?"

"Signal texts can be read by the FBI."

"How's that possible? I thought they were deeply encrypted."

"They are, but the FBI can intercept, unscramble and read them. Recent case in New York. Gun traffickers used Signal, thinking what you just thought. Their own messages about gun deals and several murders were used against them in court. They all got the death penalty."

After taking a sip, "Shit. Didn't know that."

"Read about it in Forbes."

"You read Forbes?"

Flicking some ash from his cigar. "I read everything. As my brain was healing, reading helped make it stronger quicker. I've always been a reader. Now more so."

"You should consider becoming a lawyer."

"Nope. No way. Don't have the stomach for it. Or the patience. Hate red tape. Besides, there's a reason there are so many bad lawyer jokes."

"Funny you should say that. Heard a good one last week. A lawyer wakes from surgery and noticing it was daytime, asks the nurse why the blinds were drawn. She says, 'There's a fire across the street and we didn't want you to think you'd died.'"

Filling his mouth with cigar smoke and blowing it into the sky, John said, "I think it was the comedian Steven Wright who said that 99% of lawyers give the rest a bad name." Puffing and pondering for a few minutes, he added, "Burner phones. Numbers only you and I know. But we don't make phone calls. Only use Twitter. Some texting. But only use it to call if the world is ending.

As he refilled his glass, "Twitter is a very crowded social platform. We won't be noticed. We can communicate indirectly via Tweets, not quite in code, which could get cumbersome, but just veiled enough to seem innocuous. Like the weather. Or fishing. Or birds migrating. We'll also need to keep the burner phones shut off with the batteries removed when we're not using them."

"Why is that?"

"If the FBI ever does catch on to what we're doing, extremely doubtful, but if they do, they won't be able to triangulate either phone's location with cell towers. They may get a glimpse of our location, but not a close read. When one of us wants to communicate this way, we can send each other text messages on our normal phones. Something like, let's chat soon, or some other casual message that anyone would expect to see between us. Remember, we only make a call with the burners if the world is ending."

Grabbing a handful of peanuts from a bowl on the table, the senator said, "That's brilliant!" Then scoffed the nuts.

John smiled broadly at that and said, "Thanks. At some point, probably at the last leg of the operation, I'll also need to ditch my normal cell, just in case they catch wind of who I am. I'll use a smart watch to track our target with GPS."

Grabbing another fistful of nuts, "Can't they track GPS, too?"

"No. GPS is like your car radio. Anyone can pick up the signals and there's no way to track an individual user, nor is there any way to even know how many devices are using GPS."

Between chewing, "I knew M.I.T. would further fuel that already ignited mind of yours. I often wonder what Rick would be doing now, what his chosen career path might have been."

After a sip of his drink, John said, "Remember how great he was at drawing?"

"I do. I framed two landscapes he painted. They're hanging in my office. He was fourteen when he did them, and, I know I'm his dad, but even so, they really are good enough to be hanging in a gallery."

"That's what I think Rick would be doing. He'd be an artist. And he'd be an amazing one."

The senator reached over, a tear in his eye, smiled and rubbed his nephew's arm, "Love you, buddy."

"Love you too, Uncle Steve."

"You and I are going to change the world."

Holding up his glass, John said, "To changing the world." They clinked glasses.

Chapter 25

The Homeland team was at the conference table. Captain Evans was standing at an easel by the credenza that held a large pad of paper, writing the word, "vulnerabilities" with a black marker when Joe Bonnato's cell started vibrating on the glass table top. As he picked it up, said, "Home office." After two minutes of mostly listening and occasional "yups," he said, "Shoot it over to me, will ya? Thanks." And hung up.

"Just picked up some Twitter buzz on the flagged accounts. Have it here in a minute." Clicking the remote a couple of times, he opened his email and pulled the text up. "Here it is. These are from early this morning. First one sent from somewhere in Boston. Second from DC a couple minutes later."

Eve said, "Canadian goose ready to lay eggs. He's here, ready to strike. Rain in Boston's forecast was his go ahead."

Bonnato continued, "As usual, both cells only on a minute or two, then completely shut down. No time for a close fix. Could be anywhere here in the city, same in DC. Wonder what this can't squawk thing... wait, he must be shutting off or ditching his cell phone. Means he can't communicate and we can't track him with it. We need to somehow get the senator's cell phone records. Is that even possible?"

Eve said, "What I'm about to tell you can't leave this room. Ever." Looking around, "Understood?"

Captain Evans said, "That's been policy from the get go."

"I know, but this could get my ass hung out to dry."

"Whatever you say here goes with us to the grave, right guys?"

On everyone's nods and agreements, she continued, "Yesterday I met with a very senior director at the Agency, who, for obvious reasons will remain nameless. He flew in from Langley. Had to be face-to-face. I filled him in on everything we've got so far and he agreed to a technically illegal tactic. The CIA will be tapping Senator Trahison's office, home, and cell phones. They're also doing a couple other things I can't discuss yet."

Murphy said, "Makes alotta sense."

Hunter said, "Ordinarily, nothing from the taps would be admissible in court, but we're now knee-deep in Patriot Act-level shit. This isn't going to court anyway."

Eve continued, "We're trying to make this happen as quickly as possible. But it's delicate, as you can imagine. Could take a couple days."

Captain Evans said, "Couple days may be too late. But none of that matters at the moment. We know he's here and we can assume the LNG tanker's his target. Let's push out a notice for our harbor folks to heighten the already-heightened alert. And we need to shut Logan Airport down. Right now."

Hunter said, "On it!" as he got up and left the room.

Evans added, "Eve, do we know what he did to the missiles?"

"Had some analysts look into Trahison's Raytheon job. One spoke to an engineer who worked with him. Said it's possible to add fuel payload, increasing range. And he could have done any number of things to the explosive device, like amplifying the charges, perhaps changing the timing for the second charge."

Sweeney asked, "What's that mean?"

"The Javelin, which is what we think he's using, has a two-part warhead. The first charge is shaped to penetrate a tank's armor, blow open a big hole. The second charge is incendiary, it goes off milliseconds later, destroying everything inside the tank with fire."

Murphy said, "Shit. Tahk bout shake n' bake... So, if he's dun both, he can shoot from furtha away. But we don know how fah. And he may be able to ignite moah gas. Fuck me."

Evans asked, "What's the maximum range, do they know?"

Hunter came back into the room, Eve shot him a quick glance and he winked at her. She squelched a grin and said, "Hard to say exactly. The length of the missile itself can't be changed, but the internal fuel to explosive ratio could be altered. The fuel itself can also be compressed or juiced—more bang for your buck, no pun intended. This person said Trahison was a missile genius. His exact words. Said if there was anyone who could successfully alter any missile, it was Trahison."

Spinning his pen on the table, Murphy added, "Even geniuses screw up sometimes. Let's hope disis one a dem."

Joe said, "I can't just sit still. I need to get out there. Do something."

Captain Evans said, "We all feel the same way, Joe. But you are doing something. Right here. This matters."

"I know it does. But I need to be out there."

Eve added, "I'm with Joe. He and I can go. You guys got everything covered here. We're only a phone call away."

Evans said, "Not happy about this. But it's your call. Do me a favor and get geared up first. Everything you need's in the armory, in the basement. I'll get you a car."

Eve grabbed her things as she and Joe headed toward the door, Evans added, "Keep your heads down, hear me?"

Hunter quickly followed after Eve. Once in the hall, to Joe she said, "I'll meet you in the armory in a minute, okay?"

Without a word, Joe went around the corner, heading for the elevator. Hunter and Eve embraced and kissed. A long kiss.

Hunter said, "Look, I know you're tough. I'm actually more afraid for Trahison. But I'm not in love with him."

"You are? I think... I think I am too. I'll be okay. Besides, I've never left a painting unfinished. So I'll be back. I want you to stay safe, too."

Nodding toward the conference room, "What's dangerous in there?"

"The two Dicks could start telling really bad, overly clichéd mother, mother-in-law, and wife jokes and taunts at any moment. Without warning. At... Any... Moment."

A broad, toothy smile that creased his eyes. "You're right. I'll be careful."

"I will, too."

Eve moved down the hall with an exaggerated, sultry wiggle, then turned and winked at him before rounding the corner.

Chapter 26

Army Warrant Officer and helicopter pilot Lucas James was finishing the final safety-check walk around his OH58-D Kiowa Warrior. He gave the main rotor mast and blades a good once-over before heading for the Hydra-70 rockets—seven green pointy heads poked out of the helicopter's right side, ready to leap out of their honeycomb tubes at the push of a button. Checked the tail rotor and boom as he walked around to the left side, looked over the 50-millimeter machine gun and ammo pod. Then examined the fuselage around the fuel tanks. He noticed a wet spot that concerned him, but didn't see any fuel on the tarmac. Normally he would have had maintenance take a look, but thought *there's no time for that now* as went to the front, around to the right side and climbed into the cockpit seat.

His co-pilot, Mel Hall, was already strapped in on his left, finishing up the systems and com checks. He flipped three switches to activate the mast-mounted sight, a ball-shaped object that sat on top and in the middle of the rotor blades. It housed a high-definition television system for long-range targeting, a thermal imaging sensor, and a laser rangefinder targeting system. All of which sent this data back to base in real time and recorded it. Lucas knick-named the system, Grover, it's round-shaped head and two big camera eyes reminded him of the Sesame Street Muppet.

Everything built into the Kiowa Warrior made it ideally suited for the helicopter's battle-tested roles in day or night combat and reconnaissance.

Once strapped in, Lucas brought the Rolls Royce turbo engine to life, winding the four fifteen-foot blades up to speed. Mel got clearance from the Hanscom Air Force base tower and Lucas lifted the thirty-two-foot bird quickly up and away, leveled off at five-thousand feet, and settled in to its cruising speed of 117 miles-an-hour.

As they headed directly east from Concord, they remained north of the Harbor to avoid Logan airport traffic, turned southeast at Revere Beach and then over the harbor. The entire trip took ten minutes.

They descended to their assigned altitude of three-thousand feet and an area primarily five miles into the harbor to circle and observe, which they could do for the next two hours until needing to refuel.

A fuel truck was already dispatched and waiting in a clearing near Logan's runway number thirty-two at the southern-most tip of the airport. Locally referred to as Governors Island, due to its original history as an island that once housed Fort Winthrop, the fort named after then Governor of a young Massachusetts colony. The island became subsumed by the land reclamation effort in the 1920s that created today's airport.

The island is now a tarmac, a Joni Mitchell-lamented price of progress.

Chapter 27

Joe flipped on the car's siren, red and blue lights flashed from the radiator grille, as the unmarked black Ford SUV took a right from Harrison Ave, headed down Kneeland Street in Chinatown. Then, in a quarter mile, a hard left onto Atlantic Ave. Eve put her hand against the door, resisting the g force to keep herself from bumping the window.

Cars were pulling over on both sides as they barreled down the center of the crowded, two-lane, one way street, Eve said, "I'm going to head to Long Island. I still think the lighthouse could be in play."

As they came to the South Station train terminal, Joe took a hard right onto Summer Street, darting around cars that were unable to move any further to the right or left and said, "Makes sense. I'll head to the tanker. I've got SWAT snipers coming on both boats. Want mine to keep a close eye on the Tobin."

As they shot over the Fort Point Channel bridge, to their left they caught a quick glimpse of the floating Boston Tea Party Museum on Congress Street, the old ship's masts poked above the museum's roof.

In another half mile they came to the Seaport District, zipping past the Convention Center. A quarter mile further, took a tire-squealing left onto Drydock Ave and then, immediately after the Seaport hotel, a quick right onto Black Falcon Ave, and came to a hard stop in another three-hundred feet in front of the Boston Police Harbor Patrol building.

Eve and Joe both exited the car and walked to the rear, opened the hatch door and began pulling out their gear. Eve put on her bulletproof vest. Since the police also use standard military-issue vests, she immediately felt a sense of familiar comfort, the weight, the fabric, the smell of it all rushing her senses. The only difference is that this one had a pelvic protection extension attached to the front that contained a first-aide kit.

She began filling vest pouches with thirty-round magazines for her HK MP5 submachine gun and nine-millimeter magazines for her Glock. She slipped the Glock into its holster sewn into the front of the vest. Joe strapped on a waist belt that held a holster for his Colt M1911 and filled the elastic pouches around the belt with its .45 caliber magazines.

As she grabbed a helmet, Eve asked, "No vest or helmet for you?"

"Will they stop a three-thousand degree fireball?"

"Hope it never comes to that."

"Me, too."

Just as Joe closed the hatch, a police sergeant in full tactical gear emerged from the building's front door. "Bonnato and Tuent?"

"In the flesh," Joe said.

"I'm Sargent Pelosi, sir." Reaching out his hand, "Honored to meet you in person." They shake hands. He nods to Eve, "Welcome, Ma'am. Got your boats ready to go. Follow me."

They crossed the parking lot at the rear of the station, jam packed with cars parked at odd angles, filling every square foot. Another thirty feet to the pier. It was low tide, so they descended the steep ramp fifteen feet to the floating dock, where the two boats were waiting.

Joe didn't need to use his FBI or Homeland clout to make the boats and crews come together so quickly. Every member of the BPD knew who Joe Bonnato was and would have moved heaven and earth if he asked them.

Pointing to the first boat they came to, a twenty-footer with twin 200-horsepower outboards babbling to each other, three officers aboard, Sargent Pelosi said to Joe, "This one's yours." Ahead of it, a 40-foot police cabin cruiser also manned and ready to go. Pointing to it he said to Eve, "And that one's yours."

Eve turned to Joe and said, "Mine's bigger than yours."

As he hopped into his boat, Joe said, "I bet you say that to all the boys."

Eve stopped and said, "Be safe."

"You, too. See ya' on the flip side."

The officer holding onto the pier pushed off as both motors roared to fomenting life, launching the boat along the half-mile-long Reserved Channel pier, past the empty Thompson Island Ferry terminal, zipped by some shipping businesses, restaurants, cafes, then out to the main harbor channel, turned left, heading north.

Eve's boat followed suit and headed south.

Chapter 28

John went from window to window in the lighthouse's service room. A growing number of police and Coast Guard vessels were cutting wakes in all directions across the harbor, especially two or three miles to his west. He thought, *They must be looking for me. There's no other explanation for all this. Shit!*

The State Police helicopter was making regular visits, every fifteen minutes or so, always keeping the sniper-rifle-armed officer, who was sitting in the helicopter's open door, facing the lighthouse. The copter moves in close and then circles two or three times before pulling back up and away. Usually, the sharp shooter is looking through his rifle's scope the entire time.

His smart watch's GPS tracking app showed the LNG tanker was docked at the Everett port. He knew the tankers wasted no time hooking up to the station's array of pipes and valves and began offloading the liquid gas almost immediately. Within twelve hours, all forty-three-million gallons are transferred to the nearby holding tanks.

It was time.

He opened the missile case, removed and assembled the launcher and loaded a missile. He turned it on and the targeting display immediately locked onto the LNG tanker, eight miles west.

He was about to open the hatch door and step up into the lantern room when the familiar thumps of helicopter blades made him pull the door back down, peer out a tiny crack as the copter once again did its courting dance with the lighthouse. *They're shortening the time between passes. Gotta' do this right now.*

Once the helicopter was on its way, John pushed open the door and brought the launcher into the lantern room, then scurried back down to retrieve the second missile.

He wasted no time getting the Javelin onto his shoulder, pointed it east and upward sixty degrees, confirmed target lock, inhaled deeply, filling his lungs with sea air, and exhaled as he pulled the trigger.

After sending it shrieking away into the late-morning sky, John inserted the second missile into the still-warm tube, shouldered it as he turned left, peered into the screen that displayed his second target's trajectory to send this missile further south.

Back in New Hampshire, he had worked out the math needed to hit the 250-foot tall storage tank holding fourteen-million gallons of LNG at Commercial Point in Dorchester. He pulled the trigger, repeating the first missile's flawless launch.

Chapter 29

Lucas and Mel both jolted at the Kiowa's missile warning system piercing their headsets, a red light on the screen's map console animatedly blinking. Both seasoned, battle-hardened vets had served together in Iraq and Afghanistan, their well-honed instincts immediately kicked in.

Lucas pulled the chopper into a hard left turn to change their southwest heading to northeast, pointing it at the radar-traced direction the missile came from. The helicopter's high definition camera was tracking the streaking dart on the display screen, enabling them both to view it heading west a thousand feet below them and climbing rapidly.

Mel immediately clicked the radio mic button on his helmet and began relaying everything he was seeing to the Logan and Hanscom towers and, at the same time, over the state police-band frequency. Lucas pushed the helicopter's collective forward and hard, dropping the nose down, quickly maxing out the Warrior's speed to 138-miles-per-hour as he headed toward the source of the launch, when a second alarm started blaring, indicating another missile launched and was coming directly at them at more than five hundred feet-per-second.

Two minutes and three seconds later, everything changed.

Chapter 30

A southeasterly breeze was blowing at twelve miles an hour, with occasional gusts to twenty, across coastal Massachusetts on this warm June day, the direction of the wind influencing the track of the decimation.

As the missile reached the apex of its eight-mile arc and leapt toward the top of the ship's center LNG tank, its first charge exploded on contact, ripping a gaping six-foot hole that opened the top of the entire tank and fractured the three tanks on either side of it, releasing more than half of the forty-million gallons of gas into the warm air, instantly turning it into a rapidly expanding vapor cloud as the sub-zero-chilled liquid met the seventy-eight degree air.

Two seconds later, when the second incendiary charge went off inside the tank, hell, in all its fiery 2,600-degree venomous rage—1,100 degrees hotter than a wildfire—was unleashed.

The gas cloud had grown to become two hundred feet high, one thousand feet wide before igniting into a rapidly expanding inferno—a raging, bellowing, searing, blue and yellow globe—liquefying steel and vaporizing everything else instantly.

The ship's three remaining tanks capitulated in seconds, releasing the rest of the ship's contents, nearly doubling the height and width of the fireball in all directions.

Next, nearly at once:

North of the ship, a thousand feet away, the closest of the two largest 180-foot tall storage tanks succumbed to the intense heat, overwhelming its foam insulation and emergency fire suppression system, quickly adding two-hundred-million gallons of vaporizing LNG, nearly five-times the amount on the ship, to the expanding fire cloud, now more than three thousand feet, more than a half mile, in circumference and expanding.

A field of twenty five storage tanks, five rows of five, each holding eight million gallons, melted and ignited in a rolling cascade, releasing another two-hundred million gallons into the air. The size of the roiling globe of fire was now a mile wide and three hundred feet high, the wind moving it slowly in a northwesterly direction, the devastation fanning out three-hundred-and-sixty degrees.

The firmament was filled with a raging roar so loud that thousands upon thousands of screams were never heard. More were never made. The air was sucked out of lungs, bodies turned to blackened crisps and then to ashen mounds within milliseconds.

To the south and east of the tanker, the expanding fiery cloud began softening and melting the steel girders, trusses, and decks of the Tobin bridge. A cascade of exploding and melting cars on the upper and lower decks further weakened the bridge and within five minutes the entire eight hundred foot center section melted and folded between its two towering concrete support piers—the thrashing liquefied mass fell one hundred and thirty five feet below into the harbor. A cloud of steam billowed as it hit the water in large, flame-engulfed blobs.

Next to the bridge on the Chelsea side, the fireball overwhelmed eight of the closest LNG storage tanks owned by World Petroleum, which then melted the next five tanks and caused the inferno cloud to expand further east and south into Chelsea and East Boston.

The McArdle Bridge connecting the two cities over the Chelsea Creek, and the cars and trucks that were on it, suffered the same exploding, liquefying, and collapsing fate as the Tobin.

The fireball itself grew and burned for nearly an hour as the wind pushed it northwest for seven more miles. Given the densely and compactly congested populations of the communities closest to the fire's epicenter—with so many double- and triple-decker homes, apartment and office buildings, warehouses, factories and storefronts all tightly packed together on narrow streets—the area beyond the deadliest three-mile inner circle—fires and earth-rattling explosions would continue for five more days.

The apocalyptic fireball finally dissipated, running out of fuel as it reached Spot Pond and the Mystic Lakes in Medford, Stoneham, Arlington, and Winchester, obliterating much of those cities and everything else in its path.

Astronauts viewing this unfolding scene from the space station initially thought a volcano had erupted in the heart of Boston. A volcano would likely have been less lethal.

Chapter 31

From their height over the harbor, Lucas and Mel could clearly see the expanding raging inferno and felt the cacophonous repetitive thumps of continuous explosions, like a fireworks finale times a thousand, off to their left.

But their primary focus was what was happening directly in front of them. They had faced many missiles and RPGs hurled at them in battle and were highly experienced at avoiding them, which was Lucas' initial reaction.

Instead, he held the helicopter steady. Mel fired a quick burst from the machine gun in hopes of hitting the missile streaking toward them at nearly twice the speed of sound, but missed. Lucas and Mel looked at each other, Mel nodded and said, "Let's do it."

Lucas gave the stick a tug to the left, lining up the Kiowa directly into the missile's path. One second later, the missile struck. The explosion set off the seven Hydra-70 rockets in their pods, the gun's two-thousand fifty-caliber rounds, and the remaining fuel, disintegrating the helicopter into many small, violently separated, flaming pieces, all raining fifteen-hundred feet into the ocean below.

Chapter 32

Eve's boat was heading toward Long Island, just a quarter-mile to the west, when they saw the first missile launch from the top of the lighthouse. A State Police helicopter arrived from a pass of the Deer Island Light. It was a thousand feet away and closing quickly. As John shot off the second missile, the State Police SWAT sharpshooter had him in his Remington MSR's sights and fired several shots in rapid succession.

Three of the .223-caliber rounds hit the Javelin launch tube, nearly knocking it out of John's hands. When he realized what was happening, he dropped the launcher, turned and dove through the open glass lantern room door. He heard bullets pinging off the metal railing and deck, several glass panes shattering, bullets zipping and dinging all around him as he crab-crawled toward the hatch door. He felt a bite in his right calf as he dove into the open hatch and caught the spiral staircase railing. Running down the stairs, the sting in his calf growing hotter, he looked down to see a rapidly expanding bloodstain in his pant leg, he could feel the heel of his foot sliding in his boot, filling with blood.

Two conflicting thoughts raced into John's head at the same moment—get the hell out of this lighthouse right now and run as far and fast as you can. The second thought was to sit down immediately and stop the bleeding. The blood he was seeing and extreme hot and throbbing pain he was feeling was making the possibility of achieving his first thought more doubtful by the second.

He seized his backpack, sat with his back against the cold, stone wall under one of the windows and yanked open the zipper to retrieve a first-aid kit. He was hearing too many explosions of ranging ferocity to count, could see a growing red and orange glow reflected in the windows above and then heard another series of rapid explosions that felt much closer.

He rolled his pant leg up to his knee and saw an entrance and exit wound in his calf. He didn't think any arteries were hit, but he still needed to act fast. He took an XSTAT applicator syringe from the kit and tore open its wrapping, pushed the end of a syringe filled with what looked like tiny white pills with blue x's on them into one of the wound holes, screamed as he pushed the plunger, sending the tiny gauze pills into the wound where they began to rapidly expand. He did it again to the exit wound. He could feel the pressure in his calf increase as the antibiotic-laced gauze balls fully expanded. He tore open a large gauze pad package, covered the wound and held it in place as he unrolled an ace bandage, tightly wrapped his calf, taped the ends, pulled his pant leg back down and stood. The pain was intense but he could tell nearly all of the bleeding had stopped.

He stood using the wall for leverage, put on the backpack, took the Glock out of his belt and hobbled quickly down the spiral staircase to the ground level, railing in one hand, gun in the other.

He couldn't hear the helicopter among the explosions that were occurring to the west and figured it got called away to attend to the mayhem he had just unleashed.

Once on the ground floor at the door, he peered out and up in all directions. Seeing nothing, he hopped-skipped as quickly as he could through the grass clearing, toward the thick trees to the east.

Halfway through the clearing, the thumping helicopter came around above him to his left. He couldn't hear the gun firing the shots but heard and saw the bullets whizzing and hitting the ground around him. He felt two hit and jolt his backpack just as he reached the tree line. He scrambled several yards into the trees, found a stand of thick Eastern White pines and crawled into the base of a large one for cover.

He could hear the helicopter circling overhead, but the branches were so thick, he couldn't see it, and hoped they couldn't see him either or didn't have an infrared camera.

As he began to catch his breath, he pulled the pack off and felt around his back for blood or a wound that he knew the adrenaline pumping through his body could potentially mask for the moment.

He found two holes close together at the top left and two more at the bottom right of the backpack. Liquid was leaking out of one of the bottom holes. He opened it to see the first-aid kit had one hole in it, the syringe of morphine shattered and leaked its contents. The other bullet passed straight through.

Chapter 33

Eve and the crew of police officers couldn't believe their eyes and ears. Behind them to the west, the fireball grew higher than the buildings that were blocking their view beyond the harbor's shoreline. Some of the buildings themselves were burning. Columns of thick black smoke rose, twisted, and danced above the flames.

They lost count of the number of explosions they were hearing, some large and loud, other less so. Each thump felt in their chests. They instinctively ducked as the second missile streaked from the top of the lighthouse and were awestruck when it obliterated the Kiowa helicopter.

As they were five hundred yards away from the island, they watched the sniper on the State Police helicopter firing on the lighthouse. In the pilot house, Eve listened to the radio chatter, a mad cacophony of voices keying in and out.

One was the helicopter pilot. He identified himself as Air Patrol 71, relaying that they spotted the suspect, a white male dressed in black, multiple shots fired at him, but couldn't tell if they hit him. The pilot announced they were low on fuel and only had a couple of minutes left before needing to leave the scene. Three minute later, they announced spotting him running with a severe limp from the lighthouse and were firing on him once again, which Eve could see from the boat. They said they lost him under the thick trees as he ran into the woods.

Eve grabbed the radio mic, "Helicopter seventy one, this is Eve Tuant with Homeland Security, we are currently three hundred yards west of Long Island, making our way to the lighthouse. Can you tell me what direction he is heading."

"Yes, ma'am, he was moving east when we lost him. We are at bingo fuel and need to leave now or we won't make it."

"Thank you. Go. We don't need another bird down."

As the helicopter passed directly overhead, the pilot said, "Yes, ma'am. Want you to know that we saw the military helicopter put themselves in front of that second missile. Who knows how many lives they saved... Do us all a favor and get that sonufabitch. Light him on fire and feed his crispy corpse to the sharks."

"Roger that, seventy one."

"Also, he was limping badly as he headed into the woods, so we either wounded him or he hurt his leg somehow."

"Good to know. Thanks."

"Over and out."

Just then a voice from the radio called their police boat number, the sergeant in command answered, "This is Patrol Boat one-six-five. Go ahead."

"Need you back here, pronto. We're calling everyone in. We need all hands. Chief's orders."

Eve motioned for the mic, "This is Eve Tuant from Homeland. We've got a bead on the perp. We need to pursue."

"Ma'am, these orders are from the Chief. As much as-" Eve interrupted him, "And I work for the Secretary of Homeland Security!"

"Ma'am, I'd love to see this motherfucker drawn and quartered, but I don't have override authority. I need the boat back. I need every officer back here now. Sorry."

"Okay, you need the boat and your officers, but not me. We're only a couple hundred yards away. Let them drop me off and I'll pursue on my own."

After a pause, "Roger that. Hand the mic back to the Sergeant, please." Eve did so. "Drop her and then get back here ASAP, Sergeant."

"Roger. On our way, sir."

Two minutes later, the boat's pilot nosed the bow up to the rocky shoreline. Eve turned to the sergeant. "Thank you."

"Get the fucker."

Eve went the bow, strapped on her helmet and jumped onto the rocky beach, holding her MP5 to her chest. The pilot turned the boat west and headed straight for hell.

Eve could see the top of the lighthouse poking above the trees directly east. She ran across sixty feet of rocky shoreline, swung herself up and over the five-foot retaining wall, across the shrub-covered ground and thick trees and came to the clearing that surrounded the lighthouse.

Lifting her gun to her face, walked quickly through the clearing looking and aiming up, down, left and right. At the open lighthouse door, she put her back to the wall, took a hard look into the woods to her left, scanning for movement. Nothing.

While the state chopper said they lost him in the woods, she needed to be sure he didn't double back to the lighthouse or have an accomplice. Gun back to her cheek, she spun into the doorway, head and gun aiming in all directions. At the tower, pointing her gun upward, she walked quickly up the spiral stairs and into the watch room. It was clear, just a few items on the floor. She then went out and up the stairs to the lantern room. She spotted some blood on the stairs on her way though the open hatch and out onto the deck. She made a quick trip all the way around the deck, and kept an eye on the ground and tree line below.

All clear. She let go of the MP5 and let it hang free as she went over to the Javelin lying on the deck grate. She moved the launcher with her foot. Noticing the three bullet holes through the tube, "Close, but no cigar."

Eve entered the lantern room, shattered glass crunched under her boots, some pieces blood splattered. Down the stairs and into the watch room. A half-empty bottle of water, a couple of power bar wrappers on one side of the room. On the other side, near the doorway, the empty, open missile case, a puddle of blood, an empty XSTAT applicator, its plastic wrapping and some empty gauze pads and bandage packages.

She went quickly down the stairs and back out the front door. Gun to her cheek, she started running through the clearing and into the woods, slowed to a fast walk along a well-worn path that became a wider asphalt road.

After the helicopter left, John crawled out from under the pine tree and started limp-hopping as quickly as he could, his leg throbbing, the pain growing with every step, and was now about halfway along the Hitchcock Fort.

The fort is roughly a thousand feet end-to-end, situated in a northwest-southeast orientation on the island. Built to face directly into the middle of the harbor and give its long-since-removed ten-inch guns ideal positioning to defend against sea-faring foe.

He needed to stop and rest his leg. The fort's walls along the front and back sides zigzagged steeply in and out. The construction accommodated the row of turrets where the guns once rested. The design allowed each of the five large cannons enough room to turn a full 180-degrees without bumping into each other.

John picked a spot where a portion of the wall provided a corner to sit behind, out of view from the road and where he still had tree cover. Even though it had been a while since any helicopters came back, he still didn't want to risk exposure from the air.

He slipped his backpack off and placed it and his Glock on the ground, sat next to them with his back against the cold concrete. He swallowed four ibuprofen and washed them down with the last of his water. He then put the backpack under his right leg to elevate it.

He closed his eyes. As his breathing began returning to normal, he heard a twig snap. He picked up his gun and peered around the corner to see Eve, walking cautiously toward him, gun at her cheek, sweeping left and right, about a hundred and fifty feet away. He slowly stood, put both hands around his weapon. Took a deep breath and popped out from his corner, aimed and fired as he had been taught. Two in the chest, one in the head. Eve went down.

His heart nearly pounding out of his chest, he threw on his backpack and hobble-skipped as fast as he could down the road beside the fort to the trail where he hid the rubber skiff. Putting his Glock in his belt, he removed the branches covering the skiff, gripped the bow rope and dragged it to the edge of the trees and stopped, scanning all directions.

To the north, a mile away, a large container ship sat stationary, perhaps recently anchored due to the harbor chaos. There were no other boats. And nothing in the air.

The tide was low, so he had to drag the skiff across sixty feet of rocks, hoping the rubber wouldn't puncture, even though this is what it was it built for. His leg made for very slow going and it took him five minutes to finally reach the water's edge. He stepped into the water to pull the boat in and when the salt water hit his wound he screamed in pain.

This is what Eve heard when she awoke.

Her head pulsated. Her chest felt like an elephant had stepped on it and thrust in a tusk for good measure. A rib felt broken, maybe two. At the roughly one hundred foot distance where John shot her, the nine-millimeter round deflected off the top left side of her Kevlar helmet, knocking her unconscious. Two inches lower and she'd be dead. The vest stopped the two rounds to her chest. But what she felt most was anger. Raging anger.

Angry that he got the drop on her. Angry that she didn't see him first. Angry that she didn't even get off a single shot.

She started running toward the direction of the yell, winced at the pain in her chest and slowed just a bit. She heard an outboard motor start, throttle up and begin moving quickly away.

Eve got to the shore in time to see the black skiff roughly a thousand feet away heading southeast, she raised her MP5, flicked the switch to full auto and pulled the trigger.

In 2.3 seconds, all thirty rounds in the magazine went hurtling toward the boat at thirteen hundred feet-per-second. She removed the empty magazine, reloaded and fired off another thirty rounds and repeated this process two more times, even after the boat was only a dot on the horizon and well out of range.

John heard bullets whizzing past him and turned back to look, astounded that either the cop he shot was still alive, or had been joined by another. He sat on the skiff's floor and slouched down, turned the throttle more, but it was already at full. A couple of bullets ricocheted off the motor. He felt at least two rounds hit the left rubber pylon.

John reached the lower southwestern tip of Gallops Island, went around the massive breaker wall's stones, which also served to help shield the boat from view of the main harbor channel. He was relieved it was still tied to the dock, bobbing with the waves and swells.

As he came alongside the boat, the left side of his skiff was so deflated, water started coming in over the side. He threw his backpack and gun into the boat as the weight of the outboard motor pulled the skiff under the water. John barely got his hands on the boat's right gunnel as the skiff sank, dipping him into the ocean up to his thighs, salt once again searing his bullet wound, causing him to yelp as he pulled himself up and into the boat.

Chapter 34

Senator Trahison and Trevor Brock, his chief of staff, were glued to the television screen. Trevor was at the round mahogany conference table, the large flat screen mounted to the dark wood-paneled wall directly above it. The senator was watching from his desk at the other end of his office.

The scenes of the unfolding disaster in Boston were horrific. It had been several hours since the gas fireball finally burned itself out, but the sky was still shrouded in smoke from so many still-burning fires at, and well beyond, the three-mile periphery of ground zero.

Ongoing explosions and raging blazes were making it impossible for fire, rescue and National Guard personnel and equipment to get close. Home heating fuel tanks and natural gas pipelines were exploding in houses and office buildings and blowing holes in streets. Gas stations and their underground storage tanks become bombs that cratered and flattened surrounding buildings and houses. And hundreds of cars, many still burning, were frozen in place and time.

Medivac choppers were given priority. Military and hospital helicopters, fire departments and other volunteers came from all over the state, New England, and many other parts of the country to help. Air traffic was being controlled out of the tower at Hanscom Air Force Base, since Logan remained closed and evacuated.

Early drone footage of ground zero, the gas cloud's epicenter, showed nothing but ash in a three-mile, tear-shaped zone. Everything had vaporized or liquefied instantly in a blue-yellow fireball that, at its peak, reached a mile in circumference, soared a thousand feet high, and grew hotter than a steel-forging furnace.

Outside of the three mile dead zone, firefighting and emergency medical triage, wherever possible, was taking place. The wounded who were determined less likely to make it were sent to hospitals without burn units and those who stood a chance of surviving were flown to hospitals equipped to care for them. They were being flown to the western part of the state, south as far as Connecticut, New York, New Jersey and Pennsylvania, and north into New Hampshire, Vermont and Maine as the number of injured multiplied by the minute.

The dead will have to wait. A lot of dead will end up doing a lot of waiting. The only way to identify any remains within ground zero will be DNA. And it could take years to go through entire cities and towns of ash, where nothing is distinguishable, nothing identifiable in the vast, barren ocean of gray, still-smoldering, moonscape dust.

The newscaster said the still-raging fires in so many large areas at once is making it impossible for enough help to arrive to meet the overwhelmingly crushing needs. Occasional cries for help could be heard amid ongoing explosions, coming from somewhere within miles of thick smoke and ember-shrouded air.

Some drone coverage of Logan showed an eerily still, badly damaged airport. The fire cloud had reached the jet fuel depot, liquefied its two tanks, adding 10,000 gallons of the refined kerosene mixture to the inferno, completely destroying everything located on the airport's northwest corner, including State Police Station F, Delta and Jet Blue's maintenance buildings, the airport's electric vehicle charging building, the car rental facility, and even a British Airways Airbus A320 that was parked nearby at one of Terminal E's gates, which in turn set that section of the terminal on fire.

Since the port and nearly all of the LNG storage tanks were located in Everett, this city and its closest neighbors, all densely populated, tightly packed neighborhoods, bore the full brunt of every one of the fire cloud's 2,600-degrees, instantly reducing the entire four-square miles of this city to smoldering ash.

It did the same to all or most of East Boston, Charlestown, East Somerville, Winter Hill, the North End, Chelsea, Malden and Medford.

When the newscaster mentioned the President had declared Boston a National Emergency, triggering immediate responses from FEMA, the Interior, EPA, and National Guard, the senator immediately began thinking of his bill. *Congress is still in session. Hopefully we can move past all of this in another couple of weeks and get back to work—pass this bill and reap what we've just sown.*

An item that never made the news was a phone call Massachusetts Governor Roger Brooks made to the President to discuss the possibility of airdropping water to help quell the unprecedented urban disaster unfolding on his people.

The President got the Chief of the U.S. Forrest Service, Randy Lester, on the call. Once Mr. Lester explained the immense physical danger and potential catastrophic damage that would take place when thousands of gallons of water, weighing many thousands of pounds, are dropped from the air, the option was quickly tabled. They will need to fight the fires on the ground.

President Olson told the Governor that he commanded several other New England governors to send units from each of their state's National Guard to Boston. That they've already been mobilized and on their way to help, bringing ambulances, medics, and every fire truck they can get their hands on.

The senator was snapped back from thinking about the bill and turned paler with each new horrific scene. *Oh, my God... this wasn't the plan. This wasn't what was supposed to happen. A few thousand, tops. A couple thousand more injuries perhaps. How can this be? How could it possibly be this bad? No, no, no! Holy shit! No!*

Apparently the senator never saw the Department of Energy's 2004 Risk Analysis Report that Eve referenced in one of her Homeland team meetings. The report estimated that should there be an LNG tanker incident like this in Boston Harbor, eighty thousand people would die within twenty seconds. An additional half million people in a two and-a-half-mile radius would suffer severe burns within eight minutes, and the fire would engulf a total twelve-mile radius.

With the exception of getting the radius wrong by five miles, the rest of these estimates are only a fraction of what actually took place over the next hours, days, weeks and months.

The senator's cell phone rang. Noting the caller, he said, "Trevor, give me the room, please."

"Certainly, Senator." Grabbed his things and went out the door.

Hitting the answer button, "Why are you calling me on this line?"

"We should be fine, unless your phone is being tapped."

"Impossible. The hoops someone would need to go through are momentous. And I'd probably hear about it. This town has more leaks than a pasta colander. You okay?"

"Took a bullet to the calf. Hurts like hell. I almost didn't get away. Shot a cop."

"One dead cop is, well, have you seen the news?"

"No. Maybe later. I'm heading to the second target. I couldn't see much, but heard lots of explosions. Too many to count."

"New numbers of dead and injured keep coming in. Could be in the hundreds of thousands. Many hundreds of thousands. It will take months before the final tally of dead is possible. Maybe a year. Or longer."

"That can't be right. The liberal press is exaggerating. Over dramatizing. It's bullshit."

Almost a whisper, "No, John, it's not. The footage is horrific. Entire cities are gone. Cities! Wiped out! We figured a few thousand at most."

"Doesn't matter. Works in our favor, doesn't it? Target two is going to cause something worse. Longer-lasting destruction. What's the difference? We just got here sooner."

"Perhaps. Does anyone know who you are? Did you get identified in any way."

"Definitely not. I got stopped by the Harbor Police, but they found nothing and got my first alias. By the time they figure out who I am it will be too late. It'll be over. You'll get your law. It will all be worth it, Uncle Steve. You'll see."

"You got stopped?! Shit! Now I'm having serious second thoughts about the next target. We may not need it anyway." The senator began chewing his nails.

"Too late. I'm committed. Don't get cold feet on me. I got this. And we're not on unprecedented, unsupported ground, here. Not by a long shot."

"What do you mean?"

"How many times did former President Atout call for violence against anyone who opposed him? And he did it publicly. He incited a bloody, insurrectional riot on the Capital, for crissakes! People died!

"Hell, before she was elected, Congresswoman Black called for the execution of President Olson. A fucking execution! And she wanted the same for the Speaker of the House and every other Democrat in Congress.

"But what's most telling about all of this is that not one of them was harmed politically for all their violent rhetoric. Not one of them was challenged or corrected. Not a single one of them was opposed within the Republican ranks, certainly not publically, anyway.

"And the silence spoke volumes... enough to fill entire libraries. Ironically, the silence was a loud and clear bellwether. Some even got elected *because* of their calls for violence, their cry for a civil war.

"There was a poll published not that long ago. It was actually published a couple of times. A third of Republicans agreed with the statement, 'Because things have gotten off track, true American patriots may have to resort to violence in order to save our country.'"

Spitting out a piece of fingernail. "But this is different, John. This is thousands of innocent lives. Hundreds of thousands."

"Stop watching the fake news, Uncle. The press is lying. You'll see. And you're losing sight of the bigger picture. This is part of the storm that will sweep away the elites, the fake media, the coastal leftists and their secret agenda to control America's government, media, and financial system.

"We will help restore our rightful leaders. That's what your law will do, Uncle. After all of this settles down, in the clarity that only comes with time and distance, this mission and its purpose will become clear to you once again. This is your vision, after all. I'm just the point of your spear. This is a just cause. Your words. The ends justify the means when the cause is righteous. We are saving our country.

What cause can be more righteous than that? History will say so, Uncle Steve. True patriots are forged in fire. You're a patriot. And a hero."

With his elbow in the desk, he leaned his head into his hand and started rubbing his forehead, "I don't feel like one."

"But you are. You'll see. We shouldn't talk on these phones any longer."

"What about your wound? It needs to be looked at."

"Bullet went straight through. I think I can wait until I get to Dieppe Bay. I've got everything I need for now."

"Okay. Be careful. Love you, John."

"Love you, too, Uncle Steve."

Chapter 35

"We had him! We fucking had him and we let him go!" Captain Evans pounded and shook the glass conference table as he spoke.

Eve said, "Don't rub it in."

"No, no, no... I'm not talking about Long Island. And I'd never do that. I'm glad you're still with us. Could have easily gone the other way. I'm talking about this." Waving a piece of paper in his hand. "Patrol Boat twenty two filed this report. Just got it. They stopped and boarded his boat. Did it before we put out the APB. They saw the APB the following morning and knew he was one of the two dozen boats they stopped and searched that night. But when the shit hit the fan, they were pulled elsewhere, which is why I'm just getting this now. Damn it! We had him!"

Hunter said, "The question now is he still on the boat or back on land?"

Evans said, "We're going to need help either way. With Joe lost and assumed dead, God rest his soul, and the two Dick's knee-deep in the madness still unfolding out there, the three of us are currently the entire Boston Homeland task force at the moment."

Hunter said, "Working on that. While the Presidential Disaster Declaration Bush made after 9/11 is technically still in affect all these years later, President Olson's declaration for Boston opens up some additional resources. And Alex and I are talking nearly every day. He's practically camped out in the Oval Office. Whatever we need, we'll get."

As he drummed his pencil on the table, Evans asked, "Alex... as in Alexander Marshall, the Secretary of Homeland Security? That Alex?"

"Yup."

He dropped his pencil, picked up the marker as he went to the easel, flipped back the sheet of paper with some writing on it to expose a fresh one and said, "Alright, guys, let's put our heads together and figure out how and what we need to catch this bastard."

Chapter 36

John throttled the boat's engines back from the twenty-knot speed he'd been running for the last four hours, to about 5 knots. The ocean was relatively calm as he turned further west from the southwesterly heading he had been on since making his way past the entire horn of Cape Cod, then between the islands of Martha's Vineyard and Nantucket.

He locked the steering wheel in position and then made his way down to the main deck. Opened the storage panel under the stern gunnel and removed a rolled up vinyl adhesive sign, four-feet long, and two-and-a-half-feet wide, that spelled out 'Independence Day' in gold cursive lettering with thin back shadowing against a translucent background. He removed the paper backing from one half to expose the adhesive, leaned over the stern gunnel, affixed it the back of the boat, rubbed out the air pockets with his hands and repeated the process on the other half of the sign.

He then removed a smaller roll from the same space, made his way to the bow. Laying down, with a putty knife he scrapped off the registration numbers. Unrolled some new vinyl letters and numbers and pressed these in place of the others.

While the Massachusetts registration numbers were fake, he did actually register the boat with Maryland, under a fake name, of course—a name that combined two of his favorite actors, Clint Eastwood and Bruce Willis. His forged driver's license and VISA card in his wallet consummated the ruse. All he had to do now was alter his appearance to match what he did when he took the picture for the license several months ago while at the farm.

Finished with the registration numbers, he stood, stretched his back and held onto the bow rail as the slow-moving boat rolled with the ocean swells.

Across the sun-dappled ocean behind him, Tuckerman Island, a small island off the northwestern coast of Nantucket was visible. Four miles to the north, the southern side of Martha's Vineyard bobbed in the horizon.

To this point, Boston Harbor Police have his boat's Massachusetts registration number and its lack of a name on the stern or bow. When he planned this mission, the addition of these details at this point in the operation would help him hide in plain sight.

That was also the reason he chose this particular boat model. Its popularity, particularly with the sport fishing community, meant that there were plenty of Bertrams in service and he'd barley be noticed. *Hopefully.*

Bertrams have been around since 1960, when Dick Bertram took his newly designed hull prototype to the Nassau-to-Miami powerboat race and beat the second place finisher by two hours and the third place finisher by an entire day.

The widely spaced twin 500-horsepower Caterpillar diesel engines provide ample power and allow her to spin on a dime. The solid fiberglass deep-V hull easily planes at just about any speed, making it fuel efficient as it slices its way through even the roughest seas. It was the perfect choice for this mission.

Peter made his way along the rail from the bow and climbed back up to the bridge, set the GPS for Normans Land, twenty miles directly west.

As he pushed the throttle back up to twenty knots, looking at the map on the GPS's screen, he thought, *Haven't slept for nearly two days. Anchoring close to the shore of this tiny island three miles off the southern-most tip of Martha's Vineyard will allow for some sleep and to tend to this wound.*

It took just under an hour to arrive at the uninhabited, 612-acre island. When he was two thousand feet away, he threw the engines in reverse for two seconds to stop the boat's forward momentum, pushed the anchor lever forward, releasing it from it's hold in the bow, the chain rolled out quickly, dropping the anchor to the ocean bottom, twelve feet below. He reversed engines again slightly and moved back slowly until he felt the anchor catch, then shut them down. *Not too close. Don't want any unwanted attention.*

Normans Land was closed to the public, and for good reason. The Navy used it as a practice bombing range for its aircraft from 1943 to 1996, and an untold number of unexploded ordinance are still peppered all over it. The island is now an unstaffed wildlife refuge for migratory birds.

He sat for several minutes as the undulating waves rocked him, eyelids getting heavy. He inhaled a deep lungful of sea-air. A herd of what looked to be a hundred harbor seals were lying in a giant mass, sunning themselves on the beach. *Have any of you guys ever inadvertently set off a bomb?*

Satisfied the anchor was holding securely, he made his way down from the bridge to the main deck, headed back to the berth, limped down the two steps, collapsed onto the bed and fell asleep in seconds.

Chapter 37

Captain Evans, Eve, and Hunter were sitting around the conference table, each completely wrung out. Evans' shirt was uncharacteristically un-tucked. Dark circles under Eve's eyes. Hunter's hair was all akimbo and uncombed as he kept running his hands through it. They had been working nearly eighteen hours straight with nothing more than bathroom breaks, running on coffee and anger.

Hunter's phone rang, he picked it up and said, "Yes, sir." After listening for a couple of minutes he said, "Got it. Thank you, sir." Then turned to Evans and Eve and said, "That was Alex. The President issued orders to all global LNG companies to call back any tankers headed to the East Coast."

Evans, pouring a cup of coffee, said, "Makes sense."

Hunter said, "I wonder if President Olson has addressed the nation yet." He turned on the conference room's flat screen with the remote. Every channel was covering the devastation.

Eve, who had seen more than her share of the horrific aftermath of gruesome battles, carpet bombings, artillery shellings, roadside bombs, and cruise missile attacks, was completely shocked by what she was looking at. She said,

"It's been three days since the attack and still not all of the fires are out yet."

The talking head for Channel 5 news tried to give the devastation some scale. He said, "Beyond the leveled landscape within the three-mile radius of ground zero, if the terrain was actually flat, and not its incredibly hilly New England topography, anyone standing on the burned-out North End shoreline, looking northwest, would be able to see all the way to what little was left of West Medford and Arlington, seven miles away.

"Looking directly north the same distance, only the water hazards of the Sagamore Spring Golf Club are visible. Turn further right and look northeast, all that remained were a few scorched trees standing in the Lynn Woods Reservation."

As cameramen were able to get their drones further into the ruins, footage showed mile after mile of smoldering masses of mostly ash, building and house foundations, occasional fractions of brick or stone wall poked up here and there at odd angles.

Driveways and roadways of asphalt that melted, pushed by the undulating heat and then cooled, formed Doctor Suess-esque geometric ribbons and out-of-place asphalt puddles and blobs throughout the sea of gray—an ancient moonscape of long-abandoned ruins.

Highways, streets and driveways, lanes and rows of not just burned out shells of cars and trucks that are typically left in the wake a wildfire, these were melted masses of steel, plastic, rubber and glass of various sizes that now, only by their sizes and shapes, hint at the vehicles they once were. What roads weren't blocked or simply no longer existed, were open only to emergency vehicles.

The news anchor continued, "Given the complete desolation, the obvious fact that there was no possible chance for anyone or anything to be alive, the Governor announced that the entire three-mile radius and much of the seven mile outer ring remain off limits and undisturbed until the painstakingly slow work of DNA collection and identification can begin."

As the world saw the images and began to grasp the scale of destruction, many of the media's pundits and some government officials, academicians, and politicians began making comparisons to Hiroshima and Nagasaki.

The three "expert" talking heads sitting at a round table in the television studio discussed how this comparison made sense. Visually, the aftermath of both events is very similar. The depth and breadth of the obliteration shown in the historic black and white photographs that came on screen, taken back in August of 1945 after these two nuclear explosions, share a striking resemblance to Boston. While the demolished landscape of both may look similar, one of these experts noted that the death toll is where they diverge.

For both Japanese cities, the lost and injured totaled 200,000 souls in the infamous bombings. While the estimates were still coming in, and it will be many months, perhaps years, before the actual number of dead is truly known, roughly 228,000 people died within the first ninety seconds of the gas inferno's ignition, consumed by a conflagration hotter than a cremation oven. Another 750,000 were burned or otherwise severely injured. Of those, 275,000 succumbed to their wounds. Bringing the current number of confirmed and estimated dead to 503,000 people, and counting.

As a list of each effected city came on the television screen, noting the total population in one column and the number of those who died or assumed dead next to it, Eve did some quick calculations in her head and noted that the lowest percentage of dead for some cities was seventy and the highest was ninety eight percent. She thought, *Entire cities have just been wiped off the face of the earth.*

As she tried to comprehend this reality, to grasp the ungraspable, her phone vibrated on the table. She picked it up, left the conference room, into the hallway.

She bounded back into the room five minutes later. "Boys we just caught a big break!" Hunter shut off the television as he and Evans gave her their full attention. She continued. "The tap to the senator's phone was put in place."

Evans tucked in a corner of his shirt. "That was fast."

"The Agency became highly motivated by the attack and started listening yesterday. The fire lit their fire, so to speak. And good thing. Just in time to catch most of a conversation between the Trahisons. I'm told the recording is fuzzy and broken up throughout much of it, due to some of the cell towers on this side of the conversation effected by the fire, but it's still revelatory. Should be in my email now."

Her fingers quickly moving across her cellphone's screen. "Here it is."

After listening to the recording three times, Captain Evans said, "I want to jump on a plane to DC right now, shove my gun in the senator's mouth and put all fifteen rounds into his head. Reload and do it again. Son of a bitch!"

Hunter said, "He'll get what's coming to him. So will his nephew. Even if I have to do it myself."

Eve added, "We've got to be smart about this. We know there's a second target and the outcome even worse than this. Really? How? But there it is. The Agency and Homeland have experts looking into the senator's bill. We'll know what that's all about soon enough. Where's Dieppe Bay?"

Hunter answered, "I looked it up during the second replay. It's on the island of St. Kitts, south of the Virgin Islands."

Eve said, "So that tells us he's still on his boat. Makes sense. We weren't able to tell exactly where nephew Trahison was calling from with the cell tower issues. Cape Cod was as close as we could get. So he's definitely heading south."

Captain Evans added, "We ran the registration numbers we got when we searched his boat five nights ago. Turns out they're fake. And there was no name of the boat on the stern or bow. The make is a Bertram. Thirty or so footer. But it's a very popular boat. So we could put out an APB for the make and numbers. Notify Coast Guard and police in every state along the coast."

Eve said, "Yes, let's make that happen."

"Hoping you'd say that. Already did."

"You're a good cop, Bill." Holding up her phone with a map. "The island is way the hell down here. He's planning to travel the entire Eastern Seaboard to get there. So where is this second, more lethal target?"

Hunter said, "Let's pay the senator a visit and find out."

Eve added, "On it. Be there day after tomorrow. I'm being set up with a fake profile and bio for the meeting. As far as Senator Trahison knows he's seeing one of his top, well-connected contributors. He won't know what hit him."

Hunter said, "He will after you actually hit him."

"I'll try my best not to. Won't be easy. No promises. We should have an analysis of the senator's bill by then, too."

"I'll fly you down."

"I was gonna ask, so, thank you."

Captain Evans said, "I couldn't keep my cool. I know I couldn't. Better you than me. You're the pro."

"I may not be able to either. Interrogations are tough. We can try to be as objectively distanced as possible. Remain detached. But sometimes they get personal. Try as we might, we're still human."

"I'm not sure the nephew is."

"Is what?"

"Human."

Chapter 38

John could hear the dogs getting closer, their barking growing louder. He was running as fast as he could through the woods. Branches hit his face. Tree roots and rocks made him stumble. He was gripped with fear. His heart was pounding so hard it felt like it was trying to escape his ribs. Sweat coursed from every pore.

One of the dogs was now snarling at his heels. It was huge. John tried to turn to shoot it as he ran but his gun slipped from his sweaty hand just as the dog leapt forward, mouth wide open, every razor-sharp tooth visible as it bit down on his calf, tearing into his flesh as he fell to the ground screaming.

He awoke screaming, doused in sweat. His calf throbbed with pain. A cacophony of barking seals came from the nearby beach, and two of their more curious fellows had actually made their way onto the stern. They were sitting on the gunnel, leaning over, looking into the boat. Two large bulls, their bark quite piercing, even through two closed cabin doors.

He sat up, his head throbbed in synch with his calf, which had swollen considerably. He reached for his backpack on the floor and retrieved some foil packs of extra-strength ibuprofen and put four pills into his hand. He slowly put his feet onto the floor. He grimaced through his tightly clenched teeth, held the edge of the bed with one hand and the hull wall with the other as he made his way up the two stairs and stepped into the galley. Leaning his back on the counter, he opened the fridge for a bottle of water, pitched the pills into his mouth and drained the bottle in one pull, tossed the empty into the sink.

He shuffled to the cabin door and slid it open, startling both seals. One barked as they both leaned backwards and dropped into the water in unison, making the boat rock significantly with the sudden weight shift. John lost his balance, stumbled and nearly fell. The seals—side-by-side, long, slick brown bodies glistening in the sun, effortlessly slipped through the water—headed back to the beach to join their herd.

The sun's height indicated it was early afternoon. He pulled his phone from his pocket, after adding the battery, he saw the time and the date and realized he had slept more than twenty-four hours. John made his way to the fishing chair in the middle of the main deck and sat. He adjusted the foot rest to lift as high as it could go and with both hands placed his throbbing leg into it.

He opened a browser and began watching news footage of the devastation he had caused. The Tobin Bridge was missing its entire middle section, nearly two-thirds of its total length. The remaining ends had melted and re-hardened as they cooled, looking as if the trusses and girders were made of wax. Dangling, cauterized steel cables moved slightly in the breeze.

The pockmarked, charred moonscape of gray, still-smoldering mounds of ash where houses, office buildings, shopping centers, hotels and apartments once stood. A few miles in the distance, still-burning fires. Firefighters and emergency workers carried bodies in bags, loaded them into rows of refrigerated tractor trailers.

I don't understand the trepidation, horror and regret Uncle Steve expressed when we spoke. This is amazing! I had no idea that the missile would be this powerful. Wow. I'm soooo looking forward to seeing what the next ones will do. He said, "Well done, Johnny boy. Well done, indeed."

In the twenty minutes that passed while he watched, the pain in his leg had subsided enough for him to make his way back to the galley. He opened the freezer, removed a Swedish meatball entree and placed it into the microwave.

After eating, he went in the head, relieved himself and took hair clippers from a drawer under the sink and went back out to the deck. He sat on the stern as he cut off all of his hair, letting it fall in clumps into the water. He then went back to the head, retrieved a razor and can of shaving cream and finished the job in the mirror. He hadn't shaved his face for the last few weeks and now shaved his cheeks and neck, leaving a Van Gogh beard. He pulled his Maryland license from his wallet, held it up, looking back and forth between it and the mirror, he said, "Nice to meet you, Mr. Clint Willis."

After cleaning up, he climbed to the bridge, brought the engines to life, reversed the anchor-dropping procedure, typed Montauk, New York into the GPS and it immediately laid out the course on the screen. He pushed the throttle to bring the speed up to twenty knots. Put on his baseball cap and sunglasses. Settled into the captain's chair. Placed his leg up on the chair next to his, and headed south-by-southeast. *Low wind, minimal swells. If the weather holds I'll make good time.*

Chapter 39

Eve's head and arm rested on Hunter's chest, his right arm wrapped around her shoulders as they sat on the sofa staring out through her loft's glass walls at the evening skyline. A notable lack of light stretching north, west and east for miles. The only exception were the floodlights piercing the darkness at odd angles in multiple locations as workers continued the slow, methodical search and recovery effort.

Two plates of barely touched food were on the coffee table in front of them. Hunter had a nearly empty glass of bourbon in his hand. Eve's remained untouched next to her plate. Hunter said, "We really should try to get some sleep. It's getting hard to think straight."

"At least we have the ability to think. So many had that taken away from them. Just look at all that darkness. So much light and life used to be there. More than half a million people snuffed out in minutes."

Almost a whisper, "I know... But we need to be sharp to catch the Trahisons."

"Day after tomorrow. He'll tell me everything he knows."

"It's why you need to be rested and ready. No missteps."

"I know. We'll go to bed in a few. Speaking of missteps, I keep playing Long Island over in my head. I should have spotted him. Should have taken him out. We should have had boots on the ground at the lighthouse from the start, not just helicopter surveillance. None of this would have happened if we did."

"Stop doing that to yourself. He had the advantage. No one saw the pattern yet. He's highly trained, remember. None of this is your fault. It's his. And his uncle's."

"Logically, I know all that. Emotionally, 'nother story."

"Look, I'm not gonna lie. Losing so many people so quickly is unfathomable. It defies comprehension. I'm still not sure how to process it all. Or if I ever will. But I do know this. As horrible as I feel for such a cataclysmic loss of so many lives, I'd be completely shattered if you were among them. You almost were. That thought sends shivers down my spine. Is that selfish? Hundreds of thousands of people killed, but the thought of losing just one person shakes me to my core?"

Eve lifted her head from his chest and looked him in the eyes. For the first time since he'd known her, she started to cry. As she cried in his arms, he felt the cords that he had wound so tightly around his heart and soul come undone, spring completely free and unravel like a broken rubber band. He pulled her closer and began sobbing with her.

Chapter 40

It had been six days since the attack and one day since President Olson addressed the nation and the world. He was openly grieved, humble, and honest as he spoke directly to the people of Boston. He was as forthcoming as he could be regarding the ongoing investigation, only days old. He ended with an assurance of justice, healing and optimism. It was a convincing, hope-filled speech delivered by a heartbroken President.

Outside of ground zero, on the edge of the gray, lifeless moonscape, trained dogs were still finding and recovering bodies, most unidentifiable physically. That would be the job of the growing teams of coroners, DNA experts and forensic anthropologists who were coming in from all over the country and parts of the world to help at the Governor's urgent request.

Hunter and Eve walked into the conference room, the Captain was already there, on the phone. He held up a finger, indicating one minute. They both went over to the credenza and poured their coffees. Neither had an appetite and the box of donuts remained untouched. Evans hung up and said, "You guys look like you slept. Good. We need you both sharp."

Eve sat and put her feet on the conference table and said, "Something hit me this morning. Trahison mentioned a first alias in his conversation with his uncle, didn't he?"

"Yes. And?"

"He's got to be using his second one now, right?"

"Maybe. Now or after this is all over."

"He's smart. He knows we have his Peter Holt alias although he may not know we have his real name. He also knows that we now have his boat's registration number and that it's nameless. If you wanted to travel by boat without raising suspicions and avoid getting caught, wouldn't you change those things?"

"I would. And I'd want to do something about my appearance, knowing that sooner or later, mine will be the most popular face on the planet."

"Good point. We should get sketch artists working on some possible options. Add them to the APB when we issue it."

Hunter said, "How long can we hold off an APB?"

Eve answered, "We'll need to wait at least until I confront the senator."

Evans was twiddling his pen back and forth between his four fingers, a trick he learned from playing the drums when he was younger, as he went the map. "The greatest challenge will be conducting a coastal search in the middle of the summer, when pleasure and sport fishing boat traffic is at its absolute peak. Commercial traffic also increases." Gesturing with his pen, "Even if we blanketed the airspace along the entire coast, from here to here, it would still be a needle and haystack effort."

Hunter injected. "More like a minnow in the ocean." On their looks. "What? I miss the two Dicks."

Evans continued. "And there's that little voice in my head asking how much time we have until the next target."

Eve said, "I've been hearing that voice, too. We'll be in Washington tomorrow morning. My meeting with Trahison will be his first for the day."

"Too bad we can't make it his last... on earth." Evans said as he pointed to a FedEx envelope on the conference table, "That's for you. Came a little while ago." After pulling the tab and glancing at the contents, Eve said, "It's the report on Trahison's bill. Six copies." Handing the stapled pages to both of them, they all started reading. Eve grabbed a highlighter and every couple of minutes, marked phrases and sentences.

Fifteen minutes later, Hunter looked up and said, "Holy shit. Or as one of the Dick's might say, unholy shit."

Evans said, "This passed the House and is supposed to be voted on in the Senate in another week or so. It could easily have become law. The President's signature pretty much a forgone conclusion."

Hunter said, "This Inspector General would be put in place immediately and, given our current national emergency, he or she would have absolute control of every state's federally allocated money on day one. That's a lot of power."

Evan's said, "Enough power to kill a half a million people? Why didn't any of our lawmakers in the House pick up on this?"

Eve added, "Remember, this many people weren't supposed to die. You heard the senator on the phone with his nephew. And you read this report. It was buried so deeply and extremely well hidden in subterfuge language that our folks nearly missed it. They only found it because they were looking for it. On its surface, it seems like a reasonable oversight role. There's a lot of federal money going to each state. It's easy to see why both Democrats and Republicans would get behind this."

Hunter added, "Lowly Inspector General essentially becomes a kingpin. A puppet kingpin, but still. Answerable to no one accept the head of the finance committee, who just so happens to be Trahison."

Evans said, "What a coincidence, huh. The cop in me is saying that the senator can't be the only one involved. There's got to be more. Too many things have fallen too easily into place."

Hunter asked, "How high do you think it all goes?"

Eve said, "We can only guess. But the senator is going to tell me tomorrow. He's going to tell me *everything*."

Chapter 41

Hunter was once again piloting the Gulfstream for the hour and a half flight from Hanscom to Andrews. Eve sat in the co-pilot's seat for most of the flight. They chatted. Flirted some. Hunter joked about joining the Mile High Club. Said he was up for it. Pun intended. Lots of small talk between reflective silences as both were mentally gearing up for what was next. Eve was playing out her confrontation with Senator Trahison in her head, what she would say and how she would follow up, depending on his response.

Hunter went over his notes for his meeting with Alex Marshall one last time before they headed for the airport. He spent yesterday afternoon and well into the evening writing up a report that included the transcript of the senator's phone call with his nephew. He needed to provide Alex with every detail in order to enable him to fully brief the President.

Once he landed and taxied the plane to the designated hangar at Andrews, Hunter and Eve stepped through the cockpit and into the main cabin. They hugged at the door and Hunter said, "Call me as soon as your meeting is finished. I might still be with Alex and I know he'll be as eager as I am to hear from you."

"I will."

"Show time."

After a quick kiss, they left the plane and headed to the hangar thirty feet away, where each of their cars and drivers were waiting. They were both taking half-hour rides out of Andrews—Eve heading north to the Capital building and Hunter heading in the opposite direction, the south side of the Potomac, to the Pentagon. They waved to each other as they got into their respective limos and headed out of the airport.

Chapter 42

John followed his GPS directions through the inlet to Montauk Lake. In three-hundred feet he pulled the boat into the empty and waiting docking slip number six in the Vivid Marina. Montauk Lake, once the largest source of freshwater on Long Island, is entered through an ocean inlet on the northern side.

Once John had tied and secured the boat next to the gasoline pump, he was met by a young man holding a clipboard and sporting a bright red tee-shirt with the marina's logo blazoned in white across the chest. "You must be Mr. Willis?"

"Yes, indeed."

"Welcome to Vivid Marina, sir. First time?

"Yes. First time to Montauk."

"I see you're from Maryland, so welcome to New York and thank you for choosing Vivid for your marine needs. We look forward to serving you. It says here that you are looking to completely fill both tanks, correct?"

"Yes, that's correct." Handing him his license and credit card, "And I'm assuming you'll want these?"

"Yes, sir, thank you." After the young man wrote all the required information on his clipboard, he swiped the credit card through the pump and was then joined by another young man who was wearing the same tee shirt and some heavy-duty, black rubber gloves that went all the way up to his elbows. "This is Jim. He'll fill your tanks for you. You're invited to head up to the clubhouse, Mr. Willis. There's a buffet lunch included in our services today."

"No thanks. I've actually got some work to do in the cabin. Do you know how long this will take?"

"Well, do you have an idea of how much fuel you'll be needing?"

"Somewhere in the neighborhood of 260 gallons."

"Should take about 20 minutes."

"Great. Go for it." As John tried desperately not to limp, he stopped halfway through the cabin door and said, "I'll be in here if you need me."

"Ok. Thanks again, Mr. Willis. If you change your mind, feel free to head right up that walkway and stairs." John nodded as he headed into the cabin, sliding the door closed behind him. *There's no fucking way I'm leaving this boat. Why on earth would I needlessly expose myself to the possibility of being identified. Certainly not for something as trivial as a free lunch. Besides, I've grown quite fond of Trader Joes' Cod Provençale and will nuke one up shortly.*

Chapter 43

Eve had only been sitting in Senator Trahison's office reception area for less than five minutes when Cheryl, his personal assistant, stood, came around her desk and walked toward the senator's office door, telling her, "He's ready for you now, Ms. Wainwright."

Eve walked closely past Cheryl as she held the door open and recognized her perfume—Tom Ford's "Rose Prick." An old boyfriend gave her a bottle what now seems a lifetime ago. She only used it once before giving it to her grandmother. *It's not that I didn't like it, perfume just isn't my thing. Had, what was his name... Ron? Yes! Ronald Carrington Brighton the third. Sheesh. His name alone should've been a clue that it wasn't going to work. But, had Ron been around long enough to really get to know me instead of trying to impress me with his extravagance and largess, he could have saved himself the twelve hundred bucks.*

The Senator and Trevor were at the round conference table in his office and both stood. "Wonderful to meet you, Ms. Wainwright. As they shook hands, "This is Trevor Brock, my chief of staff. Trevor took her hand, "Pleasure, Ms. Wainwright."

"Please, call me Elise."

Trevor asked, "Can I get you some coffee or anything else you might like, Ms... Elise?"

"No, thank you. I would like to talk to the senator in private though, if I may."

Trevor looked at the senator who nodded. As he gathered his digital tablet and cell phone, he said, "Certainly. I'll be in my office if you need me, Senator."

Trahison said, "Thanks, Trevor." Pointing to a chair at the table, "Please take a seat, Elise. So, tell me, what brings you here to DC and my humble office, today?"

The dark circles under the senator's eyes were a clue that he either hadn't been sleeping or was ill or perhaps both. He also looked quite pale. But she really didn't care.

As soon as she sat down, her jaw locked, lips pursed, eyes narrowed, and her smile evaporated. Looking Trahison directly in his eyes, said, "I'll get right to it, Senator. My name is not Elise Wainwright. I'm not one of your donors. I'm Eve Tuent. I'm with the CIA and the leader of Boston's Homeland Security team." Trahison started to speak, "But... what... the..." Eve immediately cut him off. The look on her face and the force of her voice made the senator flinch. "Shut the fuck up and listen! Not a word, understand?"

On his slow nod. "Good. We know everything. We know your nephew killed an innocent couple in their own home in Wisconsin. That he did so to blow up a fuel-oil tanker on Lake Michigan, killing its crew. Target practice for Boston. Did you hear that they're now calling it the Greater Boston Massacre? More than five-hundred-thousand innocent children, women and men are known or assumed dead. Entire cities are gone, Senator. Gone. The fire stopped only five blocks from my own apartment.

"We know he rigged some missiles in a New Hampshire farmhouse. Shot the welcome-wagon lady in the head. What, he didn't like her gift basket? He then drove the missiles in a white Subaru to a marina in Quincy, put them on a boat. Nice boat. I never saw it. I did however see the black inflatable outboard skiff that was attached to it. He used it to get to the Long Island lighthouse to launch the missiles that caused everything you've seen on the news. We know you and your nephew are working together. He did all of this because you told him to."

She paused for a minute. *Let that sink in, you piece of shit.* "We know you and John use burner phones and Twitter." Pointing a rigid finger from her clenched fist near his face. "*You* orchestrated all of this. And while you didn't plan for this many people to die horrific deaths, the fact that they did die is all on you. One death, Senator, is one too many. More than half a million souls are calling out *your* name. And we also know why.

"We know all about H.R.7174 and what it was supposed to do once it became law. Which will now never happen. The President is being briefed as we speak. CIA analysts found your extremely well-hidden national emergency-triggered oversight control clause."

The senator managed, "I can't believe... years... work... all those... dead... for nothing." With each word, the senator was turning paler, sinking further into his seat, as if the words were anvils falling on his head and shoulders.

Beads of sweat were forming on his forehead. He was gasping for breaths, looking a bit like a freshly caught and boated bass.

"That's what we do know. What we don't know, and what you are going to tell me right here and now is this— What's the second target and when? Who else is part of this seditious conspiracy? We know there are others, Senator. Tell me! I want names!"

"I... how... You wiretapped... my phone?"

"Bet your ass we did."

"None of it can be—" Eve cut him off, "No. You don't get to play the non-admissible card. That's off the table. You are a terrorist. A mass murderer. And a traitor to the nation you swore an oath to serve and protect. Has it dawned on you yet that you exterminated half a million of your fellow citizens? Just one of those atrocities carries the death penalty, Senator. Too bad we can only kill you once."

Leaning in to get closer to the senator's face, her voice taut, "And your nephew nearly killed me... Know this, I'll have a front-row seat when they pump your veins full of the killer cocktail as you take the stainless-steel ride. I'll see you gasp your last breath. I'll watch your foot's last twitch. It's taking every fiber in my being and every iota of my willpower to keep myself from jumping out of this chair and ripping your head off with my bare hands. So I want answers. And I want them now."

How is it possible for him to actually look worse? His face, nearly as white as the sheets of paper on the table in front of him, was now completely covered in sweat. He grabbed his left shoulder with his right hand. "I'm not feeling so..." his hand went from his shoulder to his chest, grimacing, he lost consciousness and dropped from his chair, falling to the floor face-first.

"Shit!" Eve turned him onto his back, started CPR and yelled for help. Cheryl pulled open the door, stepping in to the office said, "Oh, my God!"

Eve said, "Call 911!" Cheryl turned and left as Trevor came in through another door and ran over, stood still, watched and stared blankly. Eve asked, "Is there a defibrillator anywhere nearby?"

"Huh?"

"A defibrillator! On an office wall, perhaps in a hallway?"

"Not sure. I'll go look!" He ran out the door. Cheryl returned and hurried over. "EMTs are on their way. Three minutes." Eve continued CPR until the EMTs arrived, but she'd had her hands on more than her share of wounded and dying comrades to know the senator was gone. *I've gotten really good at recognizing that moment when life departs a body. When the eyes, if they're open, go hollow and void. Almost like a switch is thrown. On one moment. Off the next. Some say our soul departs when we die. I don't know if that's true. I've never seen a soul. But I can tell you exactly when it left.*

The EMTs bustled into the room and over to the senator. Eve stood aside as they both went to work—one tearing open Trahison's shirt, while the other hit the button to start the defibrillator, grabbed the paddles, said, "clear" as his partner lifted his arms away as one-thousand volts jolted and lifted the senator's body for a fraction of a second. The first EMT continued CPR for another minute, checked for a pulse, shook his head no. The second EMT repeated the defibrillator.

They continued this process three more times before lifting the lifeless senator onto the gurney, placed an oxygen mask onto his face, strapped him in and rushed out the door to take him to George Washington University Hospital, where he was officially pronounced dead ten minutes later.

Chapter 44

Eve and Hunter were seated at a corner table at the Ambar Capital Hill restaurant. Both had just ordered—slow-roasted lamb with braised potatoes, onions and carrots for her and beef short-ribbed goulash served with trofie pasta for him. They were sipping glasses of wine that the waiter suggested were perfectly paired for each of their dishes. Eve said, "Nice place. Been here before?"

"Used to come a lot after joining Homeland and living here in DC for a couple years. Great food, as you'll see. Love their Eastern European menu—dishes from Yugoslavia, Romania and Moldova. Reminds me of my grandmother's cooking. And it's a nice change of pace as DC restaurants go."

"Well, it certainly smells amazing in here. Could become my second favorite aroma. I didn't realize how hungry I am."

"Me, too… Second favorite? What's first?"

"The smell of baking bread goes straight to my soul." As she said this an image filled her mind—a short, stocky, full-breasted woman in a well-worn, flowered canvas apron, her long white hair haphazardly pulled back and bound by a red scrunchie, the loose flesh under her arms shook in time with the dough she was fiercely kneading on a white-marble kitchen countertop.

They initially planned to take the Gulfstream back to Boston that afternoon, but with Senator Trahison's sudden death, Eve had to spend a few hours going over what happened, repeating her story several times, first to the Capital police, then to the Metro DC officers called to the scene and finally to the investigating detectives.

The whole time she maintained her CIA-developed background and persona as Elise Wainwright, wealthy philanthropist from Rhode Island. She played the part all morning and afternoon, which, on top of everything else, wore her out. Then, when she was free, she called her boss at the Agency and filled him in as well. So they decided to book a room at the Washington Plaza Hotel for the night and have dinner out.

Hunter said, "Has to be the most convenient death in history. Uncanny timing."

"Uncanny. Unexpected. And, yes, way too convenient. I will say he didn't look well from the get-go. But, come on. It felt like it I was witnessing a biblical judgment unfolding before my eyes. I even told him I'd be at his execution, for god's sake."

"Add prophet to your many gifts and talents."

"I'm surprised he didn't turn into a pillar of salt."

"Alex put a rush on the autopsy."

"Good. Meanwhile we need to pow-wow with Evans when we get back and try to figure out where the nephew is headed next and what else we can do to find him before it's too late. Again."

"I wonder if learning about his uncle's death will change his plans."

"Hard to know. But what's likely, from what we've heard on the phone with his uncle, he'll accelerate his plan. Kick it up a notch."

"We need to find him first."

"Or find out where's he going. What's bugging me almost as much as the senator's all-too-convenient demise is who else is involved in all of this. How high and wide does it reach?"

The waiter arrived with their dishes and after placing them on the table asked if they needed anything else. Eve said, "No, thank you. Looks and smells amazing." Hunter answered, "I think we're good. Thanks so much."

"Well, enjoy."

Since neither had eaten anything all day, as soon as the waiter left, they dove into their food. Thirty minutes later, after they had pushed back their empty dessert plates and were sipping coffee, Hunter's phone rang. At the number, he said, "Boss." Answered. "Yes, sir." After listening for a few seconds, "Yes, sir, we can be there in twenty minutes." After hanging up he said, "Alex needs to see us right now."

"His office?"

"The White House."

Chapter 45

Hunter and Eve were on one of two sofas that faced each other on either side of the fireplace in the Oval Office. They sat side-by-side in near reverent silence as they looked around the room taking it all in—to the left, above the fireplace mantle, a portrait of Franklin D. Roosevelt. To the left of that, the portrait of George Washington that Gilbert Stuart painted in 1796. And to the right of the fireplace, Abraham Lincoln's portrait hung above a bronze bust of Martin Luther King Jr. on a tall pedestal. *Well curated,* Eve thought. On the other side of the somewhat disorienting bow-walled room, sat the Resolute desk.

They were ushered into the White House's holy of holies shortly after they arrived. President Olson's secretary met them in the main lobby, asked for their cell phones, handed them each a visitor's lanyard, led them to the office, asked them to be seated and told them the President would be with them shortly.

Hunter said, "I feel like I'm on the set of an episode of West Wing."

"Haven't watched it. Heard it was good, though. Won a bunch of awards, didn't it?"

"Yup. Few years in a row when it first aired back in 1999. It's one of my favorite shows of all time. Perhaps it is my favorite. I even read a book of the television scripts for the first four seasons."

"Yikes. A bit cultish, don't you think?"

"You don't understand. The show is like a balm for my soul. I was in a bit of a funk after leaving the Navy. Binged all seven seasons. Twice. When it was on Netflix. And I still catch a favorite episode whenever I can now that it moved to HBO."

"I'll definitely need to watch it now, especially if *you* love it that much."

"I've often wondered what that plaque on the front of the desk says. Gonna' take a look." He went over to it, bending to read it out loud. "H.M.S. Resolute, forming part of the expedition sent in search of Sir John Franklin in 1852, was abandoned in latitude 74-degrees 41-minutes North, longitude 101-degrees 22-minutes West, on 15th May 1854. She was discovered and extricated in September 1855 in latitude 67-degrees North by Captain Buddington of the United States Whaler, George Henry."

As he sat back down next to Eve, he said, "Call me a nerd, but I think that's pretty cool."

"Nerd."

The door opened and President Olson entered with Alex Marshall on his heels. Eve and Hunter quickly stood. Eve nearly saluted. After hand shakes and introductions, the President said, "Relax folks. Take a seat." He and Alex sat on the opposing sofa. "Thanks for coming on such short notice. Alex brought me up to speed. I want to thank you both for the exceptional work you've done so far. Especially you, Ms. Tuant."

"Thank you, sir."

"You're probably wondering why you're here, so I'll let Alex get right to it and fill you in."

"Thank you, Mr. President. We have Senator Trahison's autopsy report. Tox screen reveals a lethal dose of digoxin and fentanyl. It was in his coffee. Just enough digoxin to stop his heart and enough fentanyl to keep it that way."

"Holy shit..." Eve whispered, then louder, "Sorry, sir."

"No worries. Holy shit, indeed. But there's more. Alex?"

"About an hour ago, DC Metro patrol car found the body of Trevor Brock, the senator's chief of staff. Shot twice in the head. In his car. Up close and personal. He was parked in one of the Rock Creek Trail access lots in North Chevy Chase."

Eve said, "Now that you mention it, I never saw Trevor again after I sent him looking for a defibrillator. Wait... This means someone knew who I really am and when I'd be coming to see the senator. But how's that possible? Apart for the one or two CIA colleagues who set it up, no one outside of this room and Captain Evans knew about any of this."

Alex said, "That's why we took your phones when you arrived. They're being checked for bugs as we speak. So are your cars, homes, and offices. And we're doing the same in Boston with Captain Evans."

Eve said, "So... Trevor poisons the senator and someone felt he was now a liability, a loose end to be tied. Who's pulling these strings and loose ends?"

President Olson said, "That's the half-million lives question, now, isn't it? How far does this go? Can I even trust each of you? I know the answer is, yes, of course I can. Otherwise, you wouldn't be in this room. But I'll be honest, this whole thing has knocked me off my heels. I need each of you to keep doing what you've been doing. But trust no one. Confide in no one else outside of this room and Evans, of course, once he's cleared, as I suspect he will be. Keep going on this. See it all the way to its end. And keep us in the loop."

Alex added, "Trevor Brock's death will be kept quiet for the time being. As far as the world knows for now, Senator Trahison had a heart attack." Looking at his notes. "Trevor is single. Lives alone. No known girlfriend or boyfriend. No siblings. Communicates with his parents rather infrequently. Stays in DC for most holidays, except Thanksgiving and Christmas. So no one should be looking for him. For a while at least."

The President added, "This is unprecedented historical terrorism and treason, folks. Those responsible will be tried for war crimes. It doesn't matter that Massachusetts doesn't have the death penalty. Every single person involved in this will be tried and executed when found guilty. Period.

"With young Trahison still on the loose and about to unleash something worse, which I can't even imagine, anything you need, just let Alex know and I'll make it happen." As the President stood, everyone standing as he did, "Now go stop the sonofabitch and find out who the hell else is involved."

As the President walked toward his desk, everyone said their "Yes, sirs" and headed out the curved Oval office door in a single file. To Eve he said, "Hang back a minute, will you."

"Certainly, sir."

Chapter 46

Supreme Court Justice, Douglas Harrison, was entering his office when the phone in his inside jacket pocket buzzed. His *special* phone. The one no one saw. It never rang. Text messages only. He used it only when prompted. And only when he was completely alone. Never in public. Ever. No calls. Ever. With one exception. The world had to be ending.

So when it continued to vibrate as the justice walked past the oak conference table in the outer office, same as he did every day. Always an hour before his four clerks arrived, he thought, *I'm so glad they're not here yet. If any of them saw the look on my face right now, just because it rang, I would have plotzed, as my brother-in-law was fond of saying, trying to explain my dramatic reaction to... a... phone... ringing.*

He closed his inner chamber office door. "Hello?"

"Hello, Your Honor. I think you know who I am.

"I do. Your voice."

"Good, but let's not use names. You must know a call on this phone can only mean one thing. The Hamilton Brief is dead. All billable hours must stop."

"The case is complete then?"

"Uncertain. One plaintiff is perhaps among the lost in the Greater Boston Massacre. His attorney's contract was terminated. But his legal work is quite stellar. Even if the second suit isn't heard, he litigated the first flawlessly. Our new law is inevitable. Keep this phone handy. Shut it off and remove the battery. As usual, you'll know when to turn it back on again. Good-bye, Your Honor."

He held the phone to his ear for several seconds after the call ended before dropping hard into his high-backed desk chair. He pressed and held the phone's power button off, placed it onto his desk blotter, removed the battery, and put the parts back into his inside jacket pocket. He'd store them in his home safe tonight. While he was expecting a text since getting the message to turn this phone on, an actual phone call threw him off completely.

Boisterous and bantering male and female voices started coming from his outside office, marking his clerks' arrival. A faint waft from five coffees came through the door. One of them his. The same every day—a large cappuccino with two packs of granulated brown sugar. These life-long, highly-caffeinated twenty-somethings greatly appreciated his traditional and generous coffee budget. He also stocked the energy drinks they liked in his fridge.

It was going to be another lively day with these bright, sharp, rather recent law school grads. Each man and woman carefully culled from Yale and Harvard. Always two from each school. Whenever possible, one of each gender. He relished fueling the centuries-old rivalry between these two pillar law schools. It was the electricity that ran the justice's law clerk program. And, as he was always first to admit, it juiced him, too.

Every Writ of Certiorari grant is reviewed, considered, argued, presented, and summarized. The lucky hundred or so cases culled out of the five to seven thousand the Supreme Court reviews every year are then voted on by each of the nine at a Justice Conference. Four 'yes' votes got the case accepted onto the docket and added to the Court's annual calendar.

But with this many requests, every justice had hundreds of cases to review. So each justice has their own minions. No more than four law clerks are allowed. The clerks review the petitions, write Brief Memorandums with recommendations for acceptance or rejection. Each justice then provides these memoranda and recommendations to the other justices at the Conference.

While Justice Harrison is definitely fed by the energy of his clerks, when he's being completely honest, their fealty isn't hard to take either. Who doesn't love being in the same room for hours with four smart, funny and fervent fans?

But no ass-kissing. Ever. Won't tolerate it. He encouraged healthy, open, unvarnished, unfettered opinions and brass-knuckled but respectful debate. He wants their push-back. And he gets it. Not to mention warmth, companionship, loyalty and, over these many years, even a few close friendships.

Let's face it, the Supreme Court law clerks are the ones who actually keep the whole place up and running.

But there was also that other agenda needing Justice Harrison's attention. The one connected to the phone call he was still tweaked about. He knew the meaning behind the meaning. He knew the caller was referring to Senator Trahison. He didn't know much about Boston other than the person responsible was connected to the senator. The heart attack. The timing. He knew what really happened. And he knew the person on the other end of the phone he just hung up with had everything to do with it.

These last few years, this agenda and mission had become his North Star, his life's blueprint. It was now just as important as being on the Supreme Court. *This is why I'm on the Bench. It's all so clear now. I was chosen to serve for such a time as this. Along with a few other very concerned and highly placed thinkers and, more importantly, doers. Men and women with the means and will to save this nation from itself.*

He was as passionately dedicated to this cause as he was to being a stellar justice. At one point, shortly after he was confirmed to the Supreme Court, he didn't want to simply occupy the Bench for the rest of his life, he wanted to become an historically acknowledged justice—one whose opinions would be precedent-setting references. Constitutional illuminations. Timeless pieces of articulate legal logic.

But now this mission matters more. I'll still be a historic justice, but very few people will know how much history I'm actually shaping. But I'll know. That's what really matters. I'll know.

Chapter 47

John had been at the helm for nearly ten hours without a break since leaving the Montauk marina, so he pointed the *Independence Day* toward Jones Beach State Park at the southern tip of Long Island to lay anchor for a spell. The New Jersey border was only ten miles further south. *So far, so very good. Travelled more than two-hundred miles in relatively calm seas, with only the occasional set of notable wave swells big enough to cause me to turn into them. Hope it continues to be this easy.*

Newly filled gas tanks are certainly tempting. Got to restrain from pushing the boat faster. Can't risk running out of fuel for the return trip through the Chesapeake. Can't alter these refueling estimates. The plan should minimize fuel stops and exposure. Delaware marina is next and last fuel stop before Hooper. Then a leisurely cruise to South Carolina for fuel at the Charleston Harbor Marina. Right next to the USS Yorktown's wharf. Leg, keep healing. Slipping into the crowd for a tour of that incredible piece of Naval history is a possibility. Coral Sea, Midway, Vietnam. It even plucked Apollo 8 out of the Pacific.

Plan is set. Just need to work it.

But now, eat. Check this damn wound. Catch some sleep. Anchoring off the park's beach should be inconspicuous cover

among other boats. It's been a couple of days since I watched
any news. Have I been outed yet? Is the fake news media still
lying about the number of Boston's dead?

After he dropped anchor in fifteen feet of water, he
microwaved a small, frozen lasagna, set himself up in the
stateroom bed with a pillow under his leg, and powered up
the flat-screen television on the bow's wall. As he ate, he
scrolled until coming to CNN.

He stopped mid-chew as his uncle's official Senatorial
headshot appeared on the screen and he turned up the
volume. His head began spinning, hearing his uncle had
died only two days ago. A heart attack. Shock, disbelief and
rage coursed through every fiber of his being and he cried
out, "Noooooo!" violently splattering red sauce, pasta, and
cheese against the pristine white wall.

His uncle, his surrogate father, his closest friend, his
only confidant is dead. And he knew that somewhere deep
inside of himself he should be sad. His brain said he should
be weeping. Grieving. He remembered being sad when his
parents and cousin died. Recalled crying at their wakes,
funerals and gravesites. And even long after.

But none of these emotions came. They were
inaccessible. Like some computer files he knew existed
somewhere on the hard drive but couldn't be found, no
matter how hard he tried. He remembered these feelings,
but didn't know why they weren't happening now, or how
to make them happen again.

Anger was all he felt. He shattered the remote against
the bow wall. *Uncle Steve! You won't be around to celebrate*

with me once I complete his mission. Our mission. Shit! Does this mean your bill won't become law now? Was all of this for nothing?

No... Wait... That's not likely, is it. If anything, H.R.7174 will certainly pass now that you're dead. The Senate will rally around you, their fallen leader and, in your memory, pass this final act of your long and dedicated service to this country. Sealing your legacy, and sealing the nation's new destiny. A destiny I will make certain comes to pass. It's all up to me now.

Sleep was no longer possible. Ignoring the pain in his leg, he made his way to the galley, started a pot of coffee and headed up to the bridge to plot the next destination's course into the GPS.

Chapter 48

Captain Evans, Eve, and Hunter were back in the conference room. Evans was pacing back and forth in front of the credenza, incessantly clicking his pen, chewing on his lower lip. He looked a bit scruffy for not having shaved for three days. Hunter stood and stared out the window at the other end of the room, sipping coffee. Eve had both elbows on the table, holding her head in her hands, her eyes were closed.

Eve and Hunter came directly from the airport after leaving the White House. They decided against the hotel after meeting with the President. Neither had slept but were still running on adrenaline and caffeine. The Captain had been up most of the night as Secret Service searched for bugs. None were found in any of their phones, homes, cars or offices.

Eve, eyes still closed. "While part of me is jumping for joy at the senator's demise, I am kicking myself for not getting any information out of him. And the clock is ticking. Loudly. Anyone have any ideas? My brain's fried."

Evans said, "How many other LNG ports did you say were on the East Coast? And how many of those have lighthouses nearby?"

Eve snapped to life. "Captain, you're a genius."

"Nope. Just a cop. Wanna' see my flat feet?"

Chuckling. "I'm good, thanks… Only three other ports."

She turned on the flat screen, opened a browser, Googled a map of the East Coast. "Let's work our way up from one the farthest away. South. Gulf of Mexico. But it's way out here. More than a hundred miles from shore or anything else.

"Further north there's one, actually two, possible targets in St. Charles, Louisiana. There's an LNG plant right here on the coast, on the south side of Lake Calcasieu. And an LNG terminal on the north shore of the lake. About thirty miles away. A lighthouse here. Sabine Pass. But it's a good twenty five miles away from the plant, which is surrounded by nothing but acres of wildlife refuge. And it's gotta be a good fifty-mile reach from the lighthouse to the terminal."

Evans said, "Rule that one out, too."

"Next one further north is Elba Island, right here on the Georgia, South Carolina border. The LNG facility is here, about eight miles up the Savannah River from the coast. The Cockspur Island lighthouse seems to be about six miles away."

Evans said, "Strong possibility. Savannah's right here to the west. But in nearly every direction for many miles, like the one we just looked at, nothing but wildlife refuge. Unless he's got a grudge against Bambi and Thumper, doesn't seem likely."

"Last one. And closest. Cove Point, Maryland."

Evans added, "Lighthouse is right there. Direct shot."

"Sure, but it's a mile and a half away. Unless he's suicidal, it's much too close. He'd fry himself."

Hunter, his back leaning against the window, said, "I wouldn't rule out a kamikaze move with this guy, but we already know he's planning to head to the Virgin Islands when he's done. The Patuxent Naval Airbase is pretty close. NAS Pax River. Was stationed there for six months. Could that be it? It'd certainly hit the Navy pretty hard. They conduct about two hundred thousand air operations every year. Got a test pilot school. Some R&D facilities. Rumors of possible skunk works."

Eve said, "Don't think so. About a mile north of the LNG port. What's that?"

Evans said, "Holy shit. Nuclear power plant. Calvert Cliffs. Longer lasting damage is what Trahison said. This'd be Chernobyl on steroids."

Eve continued, "Eight miles south. Hooper Island lighthouse. Nothing near it. Automated. I'm pulling up some images. There. He could pull his boat right up to it. If Trahison follows the same pattern, this is the most likely target. There's nothing between the LNG facility and the power plant. It's an open and clear shot."

Off his his cell phone Evans added, "On their website, the LNG facility's tanks hold 14.6 billion cubic feet of LNG. I'm no expert, but seems to me like plenty to get the job done. LNG ships have been turned back, so at least that's out. He'll need to hit the storage tanks. Maybe he's planning to shoot more than one missile again."

Hunter said, "It is wide open to the nuke plant. But as far as there being nothing in the way, the Naval airbase is a straight shot. Direct line to the lighthouse. There's an awful lot of firepower sitting a mere eight miles away. Once we know he's there, we can take out the entire lighthouse. Blow it out like a candle. Trahison with it."

Eve said, "But we need him alive. Means we need to take him. Stop him before he can launch. We know all too well what an LNG-fueled inferno can do. Add radioactivity to the mix and, well... many die immediately, countless more continue to get sick and die for years. Perhaps decades.

"The wind would likely carry the radioactive cloud northwest, right up here to DC. There's no telling how many lives would be lost or how much land and water would become contaminated. Unusable for a thousand years. The heart and soul of our government could become radioactive."

Evans added, "With a setup like that, where's Sweeney and Murphy when you need 'em."

"When *will* they be joining us again?"

"Probably another week. Sweeney at least. Not much else they can do. There's no need for detective work when you know who did it. It's all cautious clean up and body recovery now. Mostly DNA recovery.

"It's why the same DNA specialists who worked the Hawaii Maui fires are here now. Governor asked them to help. These are the men and women who worked recently in Ukraine. Some are veterans of the post-September 11 body recovery and ID. Some are the anthropologists who examine human remains after any really bad California wildfires. Got their work cut out for them, for sure.

"And we're getting them some tech help, too. A company in Colorado that developed a rapid DNA processing system reached out. This thing identifies a DNA sample in less than two hours. Size of a laser printer. Company's sending us ten now. More as we coordinate and ramp up. Should cut quite a bit of time out of the overwhelming task ahead."

Evans started pacing again and continued. "Murphy's gonna' take longer to come back. Told him to take all the time he needs. He had a lot of family and friends still living in Everett. It's where he's from. He went to Everett High. It's not there anymore. Not just the high school... Everett... the city... it's gone."

Phone in hand as Hunter left the room, said, "I'm calling Alex now to let him know we have a bead on the next target."

Evans poured some coffee, stirred in some sugar and asked, "How long do you think it takes to get from Boston Harbor to Cove Point by boat?"

Eve, using a plastic coffee stirrer as a ruler and pointer, said, "Let's see... About five-hundred miles. Maybe six. Obviously the speed he's travelling and weather will be factors. He's gotta stop for fuel. Not sure what the range is for his boat. Probably needs to gas up once or twice. Maybe more. Boat's got two big engines. And two big tanks. He's gotta sleep. A week? Maybe eight to ten days or so? "

"We don't have much time left."

Hunter returned, "Time left for what?"

"Trahison's perhaps a day or two away from Cove Point."

"We know where he's going, or at least we're pretty sure. We can be there waiting."

A smirk. Eyebrows raised, Eve said, "But I thought you wanted to blow it out like a candle."

"The fact that he'll be so close to so much military firepower, I mean soooo muuuuch firepower, and to not be able to use any of it just hurts. It physically hurts."

Evans added, "If he doesn't use his cell, we can't pinpoint him. And he won't use it if he knows his uncle is dead. Has no reason to."

Hunter said, "Been no cell activity since their recorded conversation a couple days before the senator's death." To Eve, "We can pack our gear into the Gulfstream and be there tonight. Have a boat drop us off at the lighthouse and you and I, and perhaps one or two other law-enforcement friends, can be waiting when he arrives."

Eve said, "Let's also get some on-the-water backup."

Hunter points. "I'll arrange for a couple of Maryland state police boats here, off the shore of Hoopersville. About a mile east of the lighthouse. Out of sight so we don't spook him, but close enough to get there pretty quick. We can call them in once Trahison enters the lighthouse. By then we'll have him zipped. Then it's back to Patuxent for some show and tell."

"Sounds like a plan. With one change. We've not slept for almost two days, so we should catch some z's and leave at first light tomorrow."

Evans said, "I know the President wants answers. We all do. But it ends here, one way or the other. There's no way this sonofabitch is spending the rest of his days lounging on some beach in the West Indies. So, if it comes down to it, don't hesitate to send him straight to hell instead."

Chapter 49

All John could think about was getting to Cove Point as quickly as possible, so for this last leg of the trip he pushed the Bertram's speed to forty-five miles per hour, nearly as fast as it could go. This got him to a marina in Delaware three hours sooner to refill the tanks.

Forty-five minutes later, fully fueled, he made his way out of the South Beach Marina, increased his speed once as he hit the Indian River Inlet and then opened the throttle to full as he passed under the Cullen Bridge and back into the open ocean heading south.

Night was falling fast and he was ten hours away from the Chesapeake Bay inlet. Then another two hours to the Hooper Island Lighthouse.

It was now past midnight and nearly three days without sleep. But John had prepared for this possibility and packed some amphetamines in his shaving kit. Took two about a half hour ago. They were kicking in and so was the euphoria. His skin tingled. His body hummed. There was a whooshing sound in his ears. It wasn't the wind, this was deeper. All his senses were on overdrive.

But as his mind raced, two unwelcome thoughts hit him like the concussive force of two-and-a-half pounds of HMX, TNT, and aluminum powder. *Fucking idiot. He must have activated the Stinger's self-destruct.*

Built into every Stinger missile, once fired, should it miss, or not detonate on impact, seventeen-seconds later, it explodes on its own.

It took a long time to remember. Years. But now I recall as if it were yesterday. I was working at my bench. I looked up at him at some point. His back to me as he leaned over his workbench. The Stinger's warhead and tail fins visible. Poked out on each side of him. Like a postmodern twist on Frankenstein's neck bolts. More like Steve Martin's arrow-through-the-head gag.

The HMX alone would've been enough. More than enough. Add our old friend TNT, shake in some powdered aluminum to keep things hot, hot, hot, and… voila, four years later, you're back to "normal." Four years of learning how to breathe, move, speak, sit, eat, stand, walk, and think again. On the upside, that missile tech, what the hell was his name?… Shit… Briggs, I think. Yes! Ron Briggs. On the upside, Briggs will never make that mistake again. Nor any other, for that matter. Good riddance.

The second unwelcomed thought… *What if my uncle's heart attack wasn't natural? What if he was killed and his death made to look like a heart attack? Easy enough to pull off. Lots of chemical options available to make it happen. But why? What could possibly be the reason he would need to be taken out? Why now? His bill is still making its way through the Senate. Makes no sense. Was it a hit? Did an enemy discover what he was doing? What enemy? Someone on the left? It had to be an actual heart attack. Or was it?*

He started to wonder whether or not the Black Beauties he took would bring on one of his blinding headaches. He hadn't had one in years, but he also hadn't done any drugs during those same years. The euphoria was diminishing somewhat now and a bit of paranoid was taking its place.

Pushing the boat this fast on a cloudy, mostly moon-hidden night started freaking him out, so he cut back on his speed. The rack of lights on the bridge's roof just above him projected plenty of light, but only a hundred feet ahead and he suddenly feared hitting any floating debris big enough to do some hull or prop damage or worse. He pulled back the throttle and cut his speed in half.

Going slower won't hurt. Should be at the Chesapeake by late afternoon instead of morning. Still more than enough time before dark.

Uncle Steve, you said there were others involved in this endeavor to shake and wake America back on track. To pull it away from the brink of its politically correct, transgenderized, dare-not-offend-anyone wokeness, where the leftist states are leading us all by their ring-pierced noses, whether we wanted to go or not. There are other patriots willing to do whatever it takes to save our nation, even if it means sacrificing a few thousand to get there. Don't believe for a minute that it was hundreds of thousands, like the fake media says. And if it is, so what?

This country is built on the tough decisions leaders have had to make over the last two centuries to sacrifice hundreds of thousands of young men and women on the altar of war. Uncle Steve, you were such a leader. Still can't believe you're gone. You always honored the sacrifices the few made to serve the many. And this is a war. No doubt about it. A political war. A gender war. A religious war, although why anyone would want to fight over which superstition was less superstitious is beyond me. It's a culture war. A war for America's hearts, minds and wallets. It doesn't matter that in this phase of the battle those who died didn't do so voluntarily. Or that children and women, the aged and infirmed were among the dead. But that tends to be a price of all wars anyway. So what's a few thousand weighed against three hundred and thirty two million, after all? Even if it is a few hundred thousand. That's still easy math.

Wish you mentioned some names, Uncle. It would be nice to know who I can trust, now that you're gone. Who can help me if I need it? But you were quiet about those involved, even when I asked. Part of the group's design, you said. Keeping information and actions siloed protects the mission should any portion get discovered or interrupted. No one else even knows about me. All they knew was something big would happen somewhere on the East Coast. Boston, most likely. That's it.

But there was that one night... remember? We were hitting your favorite bottle of Macallan Double Cask pretty hard. No. I take that back. Really, really hard. You alluded to partners in the Senate, on the Supreme Court, and in the President's inner circle. All working with one or two others, like you and me. Each believing as fervently as we do. Working behind the scenes. Wait... Did one of them kill you? Was it a preventative measure? A means to protect the others? Was your role in all of this somehow discovered? Did—"

It hit him like a gunshot to the head.

The entire right side of his brain was on fire. He couldn't see clearly, everything went squiggly. He screamed in agony and it was all he could do to pull the throttle all the way back.

He squinted at the GPS screen through the pain and undulating haze. He was approximately three miles off Delaware's coast, near Ocean City. He turned the boat directly west, pushed the throttle up some and headed toward shore. He struggled to remain conscious and alert enough to view the depth gauge. He dug deep, fighting to see what little his wonky vision was letting in, trying to communicate with his non-receiving brain. He felt himself slipping into darkness. His willpower draining with every breath. His jaw clenched so hard his teeth hurt. He had to fight back. But his brain and body were betraying him. Had a will of their own. It felt like he was outside of himself.

Noting the depth was forty-feet, he turned the key, shutting down the engines, and hit the lever that dropped the anchor just as he passed out, falling forward, dropping face first onto the steering wheel.

Chapter 50

Hunter leveled off the Gulfstream once it reached 41,000 feet. Eve sat next to him in the co-pilot seat. She hadn't said much since they got up at 5:00 a.m., loaded their gear onto the plane and took off. In fact, as he thought about it, she hasn't really spoken more than a few words when they've been alone since they left the White House two days ago.

He said, "I've been curious about what the President said to you after the rest of us left the Oval."

"Not much. Mostly wanted to thank me for all that we've been doing. Grateful for my going after Trahison and not getting killed. That's about it."

"You were in there for a while."

"Mostly small talk. Chit-chat. He asked about my art. We talked about his kids and grandkids. Our President is a very amiable guy. What politician isn't?"

He could tell from her tone and body language that there would be no point in continuing this particular line of questioning. She was cooler toward him these last couple of days, something he'd not experienced since they've been together this past year.

He tried another tack. "What do we know about Hooper Island?"

"Built in 1902. Automated in '61. The lighthouse isn't on an actual island. It's built on a platform that's sunk nearly fourteen feet into the bottom of the Chesapeake. The way it was built was cutting edge technology back then. Sits in about eighteen-feet of water. It's called a sparkplug lighthouse. You'll see why when we get there. Google had some pictures. The base of the platform is twenty feet above the waterline and there's no boat dock."

Hunter said, "So that means Trahison will need to secure his boat directly to the base. He'll be pretty exposed, won't he?"

"Wide open. My guess is he'll wait until it's dark for that very reason."

She said all of this with a matter-of-fact tone. All the warmth of a Wikipedia post. This kind of temperature drop was new to him. He chalked it up to her needing to focus before an op, especially one that was this important. And this personal. He was feeling much the same way, so he stopped asking questions and they kept to themselves for the remainder of the flight.

Chapter 51

John was in his dentist's chair, but it was rocking. His right cheek and jaw felt numb. His head throbbed. Eyes closed. A faint voice, like it was coming from the other end of a very long, dark hallway. The dentist's office smelled funny. And he tasted something funny. Coppery. Salty. Wondered why it wasn't minty.

The dentist spoke from far away. He couldn't quite catch it. "Slurp, are you smoky?" *What?* Some other noises... an outboard motor-driven dentist's drill? The voice, now clearer, louder, closer, "Sir, are you okay?"

John tried to answer but the pressure on the right side of his jaw wouldn't allow him to move it. He tried opening his eyes. The left eye opened but the right wouldn't. And the world was sideways as it rocked and rolled. It was bright. Very bright. Now the voice was blaring, "Sir, are you okay?"

John lifted his head from the steering wheel. His headache was still splintering, but his vision was clear again. He felt better, but didn't look great—raw-red, perfectly outlined shapes of the steering wheel's hub and two spokes were embossed in cuts and bruises on his temple, cheek and neck—the result of gravity on a deadweight head meeting a horizontal stainless steel wheel.

He turned right. The voice was coming from a Delaware State Police boat. Twenty-five footer with a crew of three. One of the officers had a bullhorn. They were four-hundred feet away and quickly coming closer across very high swells.

Jolted by fear, John mustered a loud, "I'm fine, officer! Just fell asleep. Fished a little too late and had a little too much to drink after I anchored." They were giving him a hard eye. So he scrambled down the bridge ladder and repeated himself from the deck. "I'm fine, officers. Really. Thanks for your concern and seeing to my safety." He stood near the open cabin door. Nearly fell twice due to the waves. His gun was in the backpack on the table, ten feet away.

Two of the officers kept referencing an electronic tablet one of them held. Some scrolling and pinching. They'd stare at him and then the tablet, talking to each other and the officer piloting the boat.

As the police were one hundred feet away and closing fast, a wave lifted the nose of their boat so high, they couldn't see him, because he couldn't see them. He hop-skipped as fast as he could through the door, reached his backpack, pulled out his Glock and slipped it into his belt at his back. Now fifty feet away, the bullhorn said, "Sir, please step back out onto the deck." *These are kids. Look at them. Well, two of them at least. Fresh out of diapers, never mind the Academy.*

As the same wave that lifted the police boat hit his boat, he balanced himself as best he could, pulled a bottle of water from the fridge. Went back to the deck. Took a long pull, nearly emptying the bottle. The water felt like ambrosia.

The two officers who were not piloting the boat had one hand on their still-holstered weapons, the other holding their boat's gunnel for balance.

Officer No-Longer-Using-the-Bullhorn said, "Need to see some ID, sir. We're also boarding you. Keep your hands where we can see them, please."

As the piloting officer maneuvered his boat directly alongside John's he reversed the engines, making both boats parallel and stationary. The two other officers now had both hands on the rubber bumpers they lifted from their deck by their ropes and tossed them over the side to buffer the union.

John took advantage of their preoccupation and shot them both. The one on the left got a bullet in the top of the head as he was leaning over to pull the boats together. He shot the other in the forehead. Before the officer in the pilot house could fully turn from the wheel and get his weapon out of its holster, John shot him in the head twice. He then put one more round into each of the two others as they lay on the deck. He scanned the horizon. Only one boat to the north, a thousand yards away, heading away from them.

John pulled one of the rubber bumpers into his boat and wrapped its rope around his gunnel cleat. He then jumped into the police boat, didn't land well and yelped in pain from his wound. He stepped into the pilot house, hit the toggle switch that turned on the blue and red "bubble-gum" lights mounted to the roof, then pushed the throttle forward. He quickly jumped back over into his boat, landing better this time. He untied the bumper and released the police boat as it was beginning to strain against the rope, sending it on its way.

The now dead-manned police boat continued in the south-easterly direction it had been facing, rolling and cutting through the swells at fifteen miles an hour. Its red and blue lights reflected in the cloud-mottled, blue-green water. John climbed back up to the bridge to pull up anchor. He set his GPS for Chesapeake Bay, maxed the throttle forward and headed south at full speed.

Chapter 52

Hunter landed the Gulfstream perfectly on Runway One, the main northeast-by-southwest-oriented runway at the Patuxent Naval Air Station's Trapnell Field. As he should have, given the number of times he's done it. Although most of those were a decade ago, and in an F/A-18 Super Hornet.

Commonly known as NAS Pax River, he called it home for six months while training on the Atlantic Test Range. NAS Pax is the perfect base for the targets the Navy uses for training its fighter and bomber pilots and crews on the East Coast, using a number of different targets and locations ranging from New Jersey to North Carolina. As he braked and taxied, not much had changed in ten years.

He caught a glimpse of the barracks on the west end of the base—his home all those years ago—conveniently located across from the base's commissary. And with the proximity to so much food, he appreciated being able to do his early-morning laps in one of the swimming pools located in the Aviation Survival Training Center right down the road.

The only minor pain in the ass was the Atlantic Test Range building's location at the farthest northeast corner of the base, now off his left shoulder. It was right on the Bay, more than two miles away from the barracks.

Fortunately, being a lieutenant commander had its perks, including being assigned a jeep. Since strategic and tactical classroom training took place only twice a week, the jeep mostly sat in the barracks parking lot.

The rest of the time he drove another vehicle. Something a bit faster—an all-weather, supersonic, twin-engine, multi-role combat aircraft that he firewalled to its twelve-hundred-mile per-hour limit across East Coast firmaments. Making vapes and shooting bogeys out of the sky while avoiding becoming a grape. And learning how to put warheads on foreheads on the ground. *Dancing with angels while raising hell. Best job on the whole fucking planet. Bar none.*

He taxied the Gulfstream for a mile before rolling in front of the large Quonset hangar with the number he had been given by the tower, braked and shut it down. Eve was quickly up to unbolt the plane's door, its unfolding stairs came to rest on the tarmac.

She went down the stairs two at a time and directly to the luggage bay door in the center of the jet's belly, opened and raised it and began to pull out their weapons and gear, placing it all on the tarmac next to her. To Hunter, "Where's the boat."

Pointing southwest at the Chesapeake, it's morning sun-dappled blue-green water visible from where they stood, he said, "About fifteen hundred feet that way. But, to get there, we have to go that way," pointing north, "for about two miles to the main gate and then take the road on the other side of that fence all the way back here to get to the docks. Be a whole lot quicker and easier to cut a hole in the fence. But that would get us shot. So we'll go the long way. Our ride should be here shortly."

He noted a definite edge to her voice. He was surprised by how much it bothered him to think she was upset with him for some reason. *Did I somehow wound or offend her? I didn't mean to fall for her this hard. I'm in deep. She got to me and she gets me. I just hope I can still make the right decisions for the right reasons when the time comes.* He went over to her and said, "Have I done something to piss you off?"

"Hell no. Why?"

"Way you're acting."

Biting her lip, gyrating wantonly, she gently pushed his back against the plane. "I'm sorry. I get this way before an op. Focused. Internal. You're a fighter jock, you know what that's like. You must do it, too. But I will say I've never had a lover in the equation before. Someone I care so strongly about. I've never had to think about anyone else on an op the way I'm thinking about you. I'm on new, uncharted ground here. I'm not sure what to do."

"Me neither. Kinda scary, actually." She kissed him deeply and he responded in kind. Eve said, "We can make it up to each other back at the loft when this is all over."

They separated from each other as soon as they heard the unmistakable winding-whining sound of a jeep engine coming from the other side of the plane, getting closer. The jeep came around the Gulfstream's tail. It was a classic,

WWII-era Ford/Willys. Painted blue, of course, a white Navy logo blazoned across the hood. In mint condition and lovingly cared for, right down to the original shovel and axe attached below the driver's side door opening.

At the wheel, Rear Admiral Edward Wallace, early 50s, graying sideburns visible on either side of his gold-leaf-clustered hat. He stopped in front of them and said, "Tuant and Forte I assume? I'm Admiral Wallace."

As they shook hands, Eve said, "Wow. It's not every day we have the honor of an Admiral serving as chauffer. Did the Navy run out of seamen?" To Hunter, "Oh, what a setup for Murphy and Sweeney that was."

The Admiral continued, "It's not every day that I have the honor of a phone call from the Secretary of Homeland Security, so, we're even. Kinda. My being here and the reason why also postpones a four-hour car trip with two teenagers to my in-laws in Brooklyn. So let's just say that my presence here today is God ordained and leave it at that." Eve and Hunter loaded up their weapons and gear, Eve climbed in the front, Hunter in back and the Admiral drove to the base's main gate.

The Seaman First Class on guard duty saw the Rear Admiral driving, froze for a moment before saluting as he opened the gate and waved him through. The look on his face said, *Who on earth are these two? How high up the food chain do they go for the Old Man to be driving them?* The Admiral took a right onto Johnson Road and then in a mile a left onto the short road leading to the pier.

He pulled up to the middle of three docks in a row, their wharfs jutting into the Bay, where a 65-foot Maryland State Police boat sat tied and manned. Not just any police boat, a Ray Hunt-designed law enforcement icon. Its twin 715-horsepower Cummings engines not only cut through any sea and weather like a hot knife through summer sun-warmed butter, but it does so with a crew of five that can remain at sea for a week, while carrying up to 3-tons if needed. The boat's a beast.

Eve said, "Wow, talk about overkill, guys. That's a lot of boat for an eight-mile taxi ride."

Admiral Wallace said, "We all know why you're here and we want you to know we're behind you all the way. I also want you to know that in a moment's notice, I can obliterate that lighthouse on your command." Eve caught Hunter's smirk out of the corner of her eye. "We'll also be keeping close watch. We've set up an array of Patriot missiles. Should a missile actually get launched from the lighthouse, we'll shoot it out of the sky."

Eve said, "I don't think there's anyone on the planet who could possibly appreciate that irony more than Trahison. Talk about poetic justice."

The Admiral grinned. "Once you have that traitor in hand, we've already set up everything you'll need to interrogate him—lights, cameras, cots, food and water—in the Quonset building where your plane is parked. A doctor's standing by as well."

"Thanks, Admiral. Appreciate it." As she and Hunter both gripped and shouldered their weapons and gear, Eve added, "See you in a day or two." He saluted, "Looking forward to it, Ms. Tuant." Did the same to Hunter, "Mr. Forte." They both returned the Admiral's salute. He then started the jeep and left.

Eve and Hunter were given a hand with their gear as they jumped aboard. Hunter said, "Shit, we haven't eaten and we may be in the lighthouse for at least a couple of days. Maybe longer."

Eve said, "Good thing I'm in charge and packed our gear. You'll find six MREs in your backpack. I added all *my* favorites and hopefully they will become yours, too— Chili Mac, Beef Stew and Shredded Barbeque Beef. And there are three bottles of water, couple chocolate bars, and a caffeine drink. I sent instructions for our two accomplices to do the same."

"But did *they* get to choose *their* favorite MREs?"

A slight grin. "I assume so. For all I know their wives packed baloney sandwiches. Doesn't matter. Food and water was mentioned."

"What would I do without you?"

"You mean besides becoming weak from hunger and possibly die of thirst? Besides that?"

"Yes, besides that."

The boat's loud, throaty engines beneath their feet throttled up, and all sixty-five feet lurched forward and away from the dock in a burst. It quickly picked up speed as it headed southeast, toward the opening of the Chesapeake Bay Basin's protective inlet.

They both braced against the boat's momentum, Eve leaned closer and louder. "What would you do without me? Let me think. What would *you* do... without *me*... Oh, I don't know." Leaning all the way in to whisper in his ear, "Masturbate a lot?"

Hunter was still wearing an ear-to-ear-grin as he turned to face a Maryland State Police Lieutenant in full tactical gear, stepping over to them with his hand out. "Sir, Ma'am, I'm Lieutenant D'agastino." Pointing behind him. "And this is Sargent Bagarella." Who nodded.

He continued, "I know, I know, you hear D'agastino and Bagarella and you immediately think State Police Mafia, right? I get it. I get it. So let me clear this up right now and get it out of the way. There's no such thing as the State Police mafia." He paused for a beat. Crickets. Continued. "We're looking forward to helping you catch this fucker. Let us be the point of your spear."

Eve said, "Mafia. Funny. Felt a bit rehearsed, though. And please, let's all hold onto our points and spears for the time being, okay? I have a plan. Pretty straightforward." She pulled a folded, letter-sized sheet of paper out of her pocket, unfolded it to show a drawing of the lighthouse with some handwritten notes in a few places. "Let's go talk inside. We have a half hour before we reach Hooper."

Chapter 53

The Cape Charles lighthouse was visible to John's right. A bit further south along this part of Virginia's coast, the tall pine trees on Fisherman Island National Wildlife Refuge swayed with the wind.

In another three miles he came to the Chesapeake Bay Bridge, zipped under its tall trusses and entered the Bay. In another eighty miles north-northwest, he'd cross back into Maryland to reach the Hoopers Island lighthouse. He kept the throttle at full.

Should reach Parkers Marsh Preserve, halfway point to the lighthouse, in a couple of hours to anchor off of Sound Beach. Need to catch some desperately needed sleep. Wait for nightfall. Head's still throbbing. So's this fucking calf and fucked up face.

Dressing and bandage need changing. Haven't touched it since Boston. What? A week ago? No, nine days? Not sure what to expect. What it will look like when I unwrap it. Doesn't matter. Not even going to think about tackling it until I get some sleep first.

He zipped around a tour boat and gave a cargo freighter a wide berth as he passed Bay Ridge. He pointed the boat north as it skipped across the slight green swells at forty-five miles an hour.

Chapter 54

The police boat slowed to a crawl as it neared the base of the lighthouse. Eve and Hunter donned their bullet-proof vests filled with ammunition magazines and their holstered Glocks. Full backpacks and MP5s slung over their shoulders. Officers D'agastino and Bagarella were similarly equipped, armed and standing nearby.

As the boat inched around to the north-facing ladder-side of the lighthouse's base, two officers stood on the bow and caught the ladder, stopped and held the boat, inching it forward until two officers standing on the main deck then took hold of the ladder.

These two officers held the ladder with one hand while helping each of the four, starting with Eve—a chivalrous bunch these State officers—catch the first of twenty-feet of rusting steel rungs, up to the base's platform. They watched Eve ascend with rapt, lascivious attention.

Getting up the ladder became a challenging effort as Chesapeake boat traffic picked up. The resulting swells and chop made the team's transition from a wildly shifting and dipping boat onto the stationary ladder into a rocking and rolling carnival ride. Each of the remaining three eventually managed to catch and scramble up the ladder and onto the base. It was wider than Eve thought it would be, fifteen feet from railing to lighthouse's outer wall.

Eve leaned over the deck railing and yelled, "Thanks for the lift, guys. You'll find a nice tip in your Uber account. See you in a day or two."

The boat's commander cupped his hands to his mouth, "To quote the Mandalorian, 'Bring him back warm, or bring him back cold. Makes no difference to me.' We'll be back to pick everyone up when you call. Good hunting."

He then signaled to the crew to move out and the officers holding the lighthouse ladder pushed off while the pilot throttled up, sending the imposing boat on its way, leaving a pair of tall, foaming, rooster-tail wakes as it headed west.

D'agastino was already at work picking the front door's lock. Sergeant Bagarella was using a small acetylene torch to cut the lock off of a six-foot square metal hatch door that was lying flat on the concrete deck, five feet to the left of the lighthouse's front door.

The deck, much of the railing and this metal door were covered in bird dung, generous gifts from the cormorants that flocked and settled all over the lighthouse each night. Nearby on the east side, remnants of a large nest, much of it wind blown and scattered across a portion of the deck.

It took the Sergeant ten seconds to cut and remove the lock. The door was hinged to lift up and two rods on each side slid into place to hold it open, revealing a metal staircase that descended twenty-feet into the lighthouse's basement—red-brick walls with arched doorways to three rooms that, in their heyday, served as storage for the kerosene used for the beacon and household lamps, as well as coal and wood for the stoves, food, supplies, potable water, and any other items that the lighthouse keepers needed to store.

Eve had researched the history of the lighthouse, much of what she read she shared with Hunter on the plane. But she also discovered that between 1902 and 1952, there were forty men—some with their wives, some to get away from their wives, some with assistants and some completely alone—who kept the Hooper Island lighthouse faithful to its mission of illuminating the darkness and offering a voice of comfort in the blinding Chesapeake fog.

After entering the lighthouse, together they explored each floor, room and section. They were all quite surprised when the electricity came on as soon as the Lieutenant threw the main switch. Nothing caught fire. No light bulbs popped. When they gathered in the watch room, Eve said, "Welcome to your new home for the next couple of days, gentlemen." As she handed them out, "We'll remain connected with each other using these tactical communications headsets. Leave them on. Always. Even when you sleep. Eve got a twinge of déjà vu as she donned the lightweight ear bud and mic and attached the transmitter to her belt. Then a flash of a memory she quickly shut down.

"Today, we'll take turns with lookout duty in two hour shifts. That way we all get familiar with our surroundings and operational environment. Any boat you see with a flying bridge gets a heads-up to the rest of us. Since the front door, ladder, and basement hatch are on the north side of the lighthouse and Trahison will most likely approach from the south, we should be able to identify him as he closes in, with plenty of time for the Sergeant to get into position on the basement stairs without being seen.

"I'll take first watch. Sergeant, you're next. Then Hunter, then you, Lieutenant. And even thought I've said it before, I just want to remind each of you how important it is we take Trahison alive. Okay?" On their nods, "Good. Lieutenant, hand me the binoculars and I suggest you all find a quiet spot somewhere and rest while you can."

Chapter 55

John was running, actually hop-skipping, as fast as he could. Two men with chain saws chased him. Their undulating, buzzing, gnawing saws getting closer and louder. Suddenly an arm holding one of the saws reached forward, the hungry teeth caught his calf as he awoke with a loud yelp and grabbed his throbbing leg.

He sat up, the haze of fitful sleep slow to dissipate. Two young men on jet skis zipped in circles around each other fifty feet away on the right side of the boat.

The late-afternoon sun was still bleach bright as he made his way to the main deck. He had anchored roughly fifteen hundred feet from Sound Beach and could see people peppered across the sandy shore. Kids swimming with inflatable toys. Mom's watching from the shoreline, some from under sun umbrellas. As it was getting close to the dinner hour, he noticed several moms were leaving, coolers, towels, and kids in tow.

After swallowing the last bite of his second microwaved breakfast sandwich and washing it down with the rest of his coffee, he felt fortified enough to tackle changing his wound's dressing and bandages.

John went into the head and removed a first-aid kit from the cabinet beneath the sink and placed it on the cabin table. He removed several four-inch gauze pads, some surgical wipes, a pair of s surgical scissors, a tube of antibacterial ointment, a couple of fresh ace bandages and a pair of long tweezers. Then shoved everything over, close enough to be within reach as he slid into the table's built-in bench seat.

He placed his foot on the table's edge and began to unwrap his calf, dried blood held some of the layers together. He reached for the scissors and cut the rest of the bandage off, carefully removed the outer gauze pads. Plucked the sections stuck to the wound by dried blood with the tweezers, wincing when it pulled at the wound's scabbing surface, which then started weeping blood. His calf was still swollen, although it had gone down some over the last couple of days. The areas around the entrance and exit wounds were angry purple and several shades of red, still engorged by the gauze pellets he injected with the EXTAT syringe in Boston.

Nothing looked infected and he was grateful for that at least. The powerful antibiotics that laced the pellets did their job. But now they needed to be removed so that the wound could completely close on its own.

This is the part of the process he feared most. Would it open up completely, leaving him to start over and use another XSTAT to stop the bleeding? Did he actually hit or perhaps nick an artery? He didn't think so, but had one of the syringes nearby, just in case.

He picked up the tweezers again and got a hold of the gauze in the exit wound on the right side of his calf, slowly pulled the tightly packed clump out, grimacing and growling at the pain as flesh and skin that had begun to coagulate around the gauze was broken.

Once the nearly black gauze pellets were removed, John could see it was bleeding, but not badly and mostly from the surfaces he had just agitated.

He sighed with some relief as he went about working on the entrance wound. After cleaning the entire area with surgical wipes, he smeared generous amounts of Bacitracin into each hole, applied fresh gauze pads and wrapped it all in a new ace bandage. As he wrapped, he got an idea.

Completing his new dressing and bandage and downing three Advil, he then removed the Beretta Tomcat from his backpack. This just-over-four-inch, lightweight thirty-two caliber semi-automatic pistol held seven rounds. The Tomcat was designed and built for one purpose only—to be easily concealed and still pack an ample punch, making this gun a popular choice with law enforcement and the military as a BUG, shorthand for back-up gun.

After checking the magazine load and safety, he placed it against his calf, just below his wound and above his ankle, and wrapped it in another ace bandage to conceal and hold it in place.

After cleaning up, John went out to the main deck. The kids on jet skis were gone and the beach crowd had grown much thinner. A group of six people, teenagers perhaps, were gathering and piling sticks and logs for a bonfire. He assumed alcoholic beverages were in the cooler two guys were carrying and placing near the growing wood pile.

He climbed to the bridge and pulled up anchor. Started the engines, set the GPS for the lighthouse and headed north-northeast up the Chesapeake at fifteen miles an hour. He wanted to take his time and keep an eye out for any authorities. *If all goes according to plan, be there in two hours, just as night is descending.*

Chapter 56

Eve stood from her resting spot on the floor of the second level of the lighthouse, which was the bedroom. Without furniture, every level looked identical—a round room with four windows. All the walls covered in the same white subway tiles. With the exception of the kitchen on the ground floor and observation room under the lamp room, it was hard to tell what level you were on unless you looked out a window.

She pressed the small button on her headset and spoke to the team. "Has anyone used the bathroom yet? What am I about to face here, gentlemen?"

Sergeant Bagarella said, "First, thanks for thinking of bringing the TP and hand wipes, chief."

Both D'agastino and Bagarella had taken to calling her "chief" within an hour of their arrival at the lighthouse. "It's actually in pretty decent shape. A chemical toilet. Maybe a decade old. Works fine. I think your greatest danger is fallout from our bad aim."

As she walked over to the bathroom door, "Thanks for the heads up. No pun intended." She heard them chuckling as she hit the headset button a second time to shut off broadcasting. She entered the small room with the toilet right next to a diminutive sink, a mirrored medicine cabinet above. Its white paint, blistering and curling. Much of it had fallen like snow into the waterless sink and onto the floor.

As Eve left the bathroom and walked back to where her backpack and sleeping bag were set up under the south-facing window, her cell phone buzzed from a vest pocket. She plucked it out and answered without looking. "Yes?"

"Hey, Eve!"

"Oh, hey, Captain, to what do I owe the pleasure?"

"I take it you haven't seen the news?"

"No. We're waiting in radio and phone silence."

"I know and my apologies. But I just wanted you to know that they found a Delaware State Police boat that ran aground in New Jersey. All three officers shot in the head. Two of them first-year rookies."

"What were Delaware officers doing in Jersey?"

"They were actually shot in Delaware and their boat must have been set on course by their killer. These were close-range wounds. Nine mil. Money's on Trahison. They most likely stopped him, or he was already anchored. They tried to board and he got the drop on them.

"After losing radio contact, DSP headquarters tracked the boat. It made a sixty-mile-wide arc, first heading east-southeast and slowly turning south-westerly, ending up on Bethany Beach. Lights flashing. Engine still running. Some beach-goers saw the boat plow into the shore. When nothing else happened, a young couple walked over, saw the mess, called 911."

"Add three more to Trahison's body count."

"Make it the last three, will ya. Take this fucker off the board, one way or another. You guys doin' okay?"

"So far, so good, Captain."

"Okay. I'll let you get back to it. Keep your head down, Eve."

"Thanks, will do. Talk soon."

Hunter was standing nearby and said, "That Evans?"

"Didn't hear you come in. Yes, it was." As she started to tell him what had happened, she hit the button on her headset so the Lieutenant and Sergeant could hear as well.

Chapter 57

The lighthouse was a mile away, almost directly to John's north. He was running the boat at seven miles an hour in somewhat of a zigzag pattern, both fishing poles had line running out, weighted but not hooked or baited, since the last thing he wanted to do was actually catch a fish.

Sitting at the helm with his binoculars. A still, lonely sparkplug sitting in the dark, cold Chesapeake, waves and swells lapping and slapping its base from every angle.

He hadn't seen a single police, Coast Guard or any other law or military boat among the many pleasure, and even more commercial, vessels since his encounter in Delaware.

As the largest inlet on the Mid-Atlantic coast—with one of the world's busiest shipping channels, including Baltimore, the nation's largest port for cargo and cruise ships—the Chesapeake hosts the highest volume of boat traffic in the country.

Sea-faring craft of all shapes and sizes traverse nearly every one of its two hundred miles, from the Atlantic to the Susquehanna River.

While it made for good cover to be among so many ships and boats, John was discovering this much traffic also made it more dangerous, especially in the dark. The shipping channel was clearly marked on his GPS and he vigilantly gave it a wide berth. He couldn't believe the number and sheer size of the ships that passed him heading north and south. Up to this point he thought his boat was big. But now he felt tiny and vulnerable.

Pointing the bow directly at the lighthouse, he cut his speed to three-miles an hour, climbed down from the bridge, reeled in each of the two fishing poles and placed them back in their gunnel holders in each stern corner. Back to the bridge, he pushed the throttle forward slightly. Left his running lights off.

* * *

D'agastino's voice came through the team's ear buds, "Hey, folks, I've got another flybridge. A thirty-or-so footer. Directly south, heading toward us. This one appears to be fishing, trolling actually, getting closer. So far, I see only see one person aboard."

Eve asked, "How many does this one make?"

"Twelve so far. But all of those had at least two people. Most had several. This guy appears to be alone.

"Lucky thirteen. Registration number and name on the stern?"

"Haven't been able to get a look at the stern yet. And the registration is a Maryland number." He rattled it off, then said, "Bags, this one is worth a call in to central on your cell. Let's see who this is."

Eve said, "Bags?"

The Sergeant said, "Short for Bagarella. Everyone uses it. Feel free, chief. Calling now."

D'agastino added, "Here's something interesting, gang. I'm looking at him looking at us. Chicago Blackhawks baseball hat. Van dyke beard. Brown. Not much else to see. He just put the binocs down and turned his boat back toward us, making another zig. Or is it a zag? Whoa, he just had to cut into some high swells. Got a good look at the stern."

Eve said, "Make sure you're completely out of sight, Lieutenant."

"Already moved away from the south-facing window to the east side. I can see him, but he won't see me."

The Lieutenant continued, "Did we start a pool on the name of the boat Trahison may now be using? If so, and if you had *Independence Day*, then, ding, ding, ding, you're our lucky winner!"

Bagarella chimed in, "Boat is registered to a Clint Willis, address is a PO box in Maryland."

Hunter said, "I think it's him. We should get into position. Sergeant, you on the basement stairs?"

"Making my way. Be ready in two."

"Eve, I'm heading down to the first level."

Eve replied, "Already here. Just locked the door behind the sergeant. Don't want Trahison to think anyone's here. Unlocked door might do that. Lieutenant, where's he now?"

"Switching to night vision... Lost him behind a freighter. God those suckers are huge. Got him. His running lights are still off. A bit risky with all this traffic. Got a bead on him now. Definitely heading this way. About a hundred yards. If it's him, we'll know in a minute."

* * *

The horizon looked clear in all directions through his binoculars. *Lots of boat traffic, which I expected. No police or Coast Guard anywhere, which I hoped for. So why am I so suspicious? Get a grip and let's get it done!*

Many of the pleasure boats had thinned out, returning to their docks and slips or boat ramps before complete nightfall. Their running and mast lights headed toward an inlet on the western shore, like a gathering of fireflies gliding across the water.

Cruise ships made their way north and south, to and from Baltimore in the south and Annapolis further north. One passed right next to him. *Holy shit! It's a floating ten-story hotel. Wouldn't be caught dead on one of those things. Hell no! Got to be 250-feet high. How can something that top heavy not tip over when a decent wave hits it? Just don't get the appeal. No thanks. Like my hotels on terra firma.*

Commercial vessels were also riding the shipping channel north and south. After the cruise ship passed, two huge vessels steamed by rather closely, their wakes significantly rocked John's boat. One was so high it forced him to turn into it to keep it from broadsiding and possibly swamping the Bertram.

A three hundred-foot bulk cargo ship, the *Marian Invocation*, flying a Greek flag, headed south. Its full cargo holds made the ship sit low in the water. On the right, close to the lighthouse, a massive crude oil tanker, the *Oceanic Fortitude*, made its way north at a good clip. A local twenty-foot tugboat, the *Capn' Dalen*, buzzed the lighthouse on the eastern side heading northwest. The combined wakes of these vessels created waves that hit the lighthouse at all angles, two or three nearly breached the railing, twenty feet above the Bay's surface.

With all of this traffic chop knocking him around and causing him to keep the bow pointing into the larger swells, he became concerned about docking to the lighthouse and the potential serious damage it could cause. *No choice. Gotta' make it work. Hopefully, the boat will survive. Either way, show time.*

Once he got to the lighthouse, he did a complete, slow run all the way around. On the second pass he cut the speed to a crawl and headed for the lighthouse's ladder.

* * *

Through the headset, Lieutenant D'agastino said, "Okay folks, sit tight. Here he comes."

Eve replied, "Remember, cool heads. We need him alive."

* * *

John tossed two rubber bumpers over the side of the flying bridge before heading down to the main deck to toss three more over the right gunnel. Back to the bridge, he maneuvered the boat right next to the ladder, shut the engines down as he grabbed hold of the lighthouse ladder with both hands. He held on as he made his way back down from the bridge without letting go and then, once on the main deck, secured the bow and stern lines to the ladder's bottom rung.

The boat traffic had quieted some and the chop and wakes were now just two or three-foot swells that rolled and rocked his boat.

Satisfied that the lines were secure and the bumpers in the right places, he went into the cabin, back to the stateroom, pulled up the mattress and from the hidden panel, retrieved the last of his missile cases and brought it out to the main deck.

At the rear gunnel he retrieved a large bundle of one-inch nylon rope and a two-foot wooden-handled fish grappling hook. He tied one end of the rope to the case handle. Then tied the grappling hook to the other end of the rope, spun it around like a cowboy with a lasso and threw it up and over the lighthouse base's metal railing, taking twenty of the fifty feet of yellow rope with it.

It was getting harder to see as the last reflected light across the partly cloudy sky was winking out. Back to the cabin, his Glock went from the table into his backpack. He removed and donned a pair of leather work gloves, then shouldered the pack once back on deck.

John caught hold of the ladder and began climbing. He felt quite exposed and vulnerable and moved as fast as he could for the twenty vertical feet. He pulled himself up through the opening using the deck railing, and stepped onto the concrete base.

He then removed his backpack and placed it next to the front door. Then went over to where the grappling hook was lying on the deck, right next to the hatch door where the sergeant was hiding, picked it up and went to the railing as he pulled up the ten feet of rope slack. He then began pulling the case up, using the railing as a pulley, stopping twice to rest, as it grew heavier with each tug. His hands hurt and his leg wound ached with the effort.

Once close enough to grasp the case handle, he lifted it over the railing and onto the deck with a grunt. He removed his gloves, wrung his hands together, bending and flexing his fingers, stretched out his back as he went to the front door. Reaching into his pocket for his lock-pick set, he went to work, mostly by feel as complete darkness had descended.

The light in the lantern room suddenly and surprisingly blared on, its Fresnel-lens-driven beam slicing its way through thirteen-miles of blackness, illuminating the area in a glow that got brighter every time it passed directly overhead, making it much easier for John to see what he was doing. Looking up he said, "Well, thank you."

Two minutes later, the lock clicked open. He donned his backpack, retrieved the missile case, opened the door and stepped into the darkness.

He took three steps and froze as two bright lights hit him, two voices, one male on his right and one female on his left shouted at him to stand still and put his hands up. As he started to turn, a third light came from behind blinding him as a man growled at him to not move a muscle. A hand patted him down, a gun barrel press hard against his head as this officer told him to drop the backpack he was already pulling at, got it off, dropped it to the floor.

Sergeant Bagarella yelled. "Hit the floor! Face down! Hands on your head! John complied. The overhead lights in the room snapped on.

Eve said, "Welcome, Mr. Trahison. Or should I say Mr. Holt? No, it's Willis now, isn't it? Doesn't matter. Still a traitorous, mass-murdering sonofabitch by any name."

John turned his head to look up at her from the floor and said, "Seems you know who I am, but I don't believe we've had the pleasure."

"Oh, we've met. But I wouldn't call it a pleasure. Remember Long Island?"

Chuckling slightly. "Shit, that was you? Sorry about that. Just business, as the old cliché goes, nothing personal. Although you did sink my dingy, nearly hit me, by the way. And, not that it matters, but when I shot you I thought you were a guy. Yikes. I could not have been more wrong. Huba-huba."

With a swift kick to John's ribs, Bagarella said, "Shut the fuck up, asshole! I can make the other side of your face match this one. Shit. You run full speed into a wagon wheel or what?"

Eve said, "Sergeant! We talked about this!"

"You said alive. Nothin' about bruised."

Lieutenant D'agastino came down the spiral stairs. As he was about to step down the last two, a loud shot rang out, greatly magnified by the room's small size and its tiled walls and ceiling. D'agastino's head jolted sideways and sprayed blood onto the white wall beside him as he dropped in his tracks to the floor in a lifeless heap.

Hunter, stood to Eve's left and a couple of feet behind her. Pointed his Glock at the Sergeant—who realized what was happening a fraction of a second too late—and made another headshot. Aiming at her. "Drop everything to the floor, Eve."

"Make me."

He took one step toward her and shot her in the left foot, grabbed her Glock from her hand, chucked it aside. Pulled the MP-5 off of her shoulder by the strap and tossed it away as well.

"Shit! You fucker!" As she sat down hard onto the floor. "This breakup's gonna' be hard to top. I guess it really is bullets instead of flowers."

"Bullets instead of— oh, yeah. Serving in 'Stan at the same time. Our possible first date. You said it would never catch on... You'll be fine."

"I was wondering when you'd show your true face. You know, I almost put blank cartridges in both of your guns when I packed our gear. Now I honestly wish I had. D'agastino and Bagarella didn't deserve that."

"Think I took their mafia joke a bit too far?"

He kicked the case and gestured toward John, "Get up. Let's go."

To Eve, "What the hell are you talking about? Blanks? There's no way you could have known anything was awry before now."

"That's what you think. After you left our meeting with the President, he and I didn't talk about his kids or my art. We talked about you. How you're part of Senator Trahison's sick, twisted cabal. And you're working with someone close to him. I wouldn't believe him until he showed me proof."

"What proof?"

"Fuck you!"

"I guess I deserve that. You've known all this time? Wait, what you did with me by the plane… on the boat? All an act?"

As she undid her laces and gingerly removed her boot, "And the Academy Award goes to… Eve Tuant, ladies and gentlemen. The judges were deeply moved by her amazing portrayal of the most restrained, betrayed women on the face of the earth."

"Wow. You're good. CIA trained you well."

"And who trained you? Was our relationship a set up from the start? Was it all fake? If so, well played. You deserve your own Oscar. Wait, they don't have a category for mass-murdering, treasonous, pieces of shit. Sorry. Better luck next year."

John, standing next to the missile crate said, "As much as I'm really enjoying this episode of *Days of Our Lives*, I have questions." Turning toward Eve, "You're CIA? How long have you known about me?"

"I'll answer yours if you answer mine. In good faith I'll go first. We tapped your uncle's phones. We heard your conversation after you blew up Boston and vaporized half-a-million people. We have all of your Twitter exchanges. We know the oil tanker is yours. Found your boat and DNA at the bottom of the lake behind the Abrams' house. They died because of where they lived, didn't they?"

"Yes... Did the CIA kill my uncle? Did *you* kill him?"

She got her boot off and removed her sock. The bullet had gone through her foot between her second and third toe. "No, but I *was* with him. He died in my hands, actually. But not by them. He was poisoned."

"Bullshit."

She unzipped the med pack that was strapped to the front of her bullet-proof vest, took out some packets of gauze and alcohol wipes, tore open several of both and started cleaning her wound. It was bleeding but not too badly. "His chief of staff juiced his coffee."

"Chief of staff? What? Why?"

She squeezed a generous amount of Bacitracin on the wound, unwrapped several more gauze pads, placed them across and under her two toes to cover both sides of the wound, tore open a roll of ace bandage, wrapped the area and then her entire foot to her ankle, sealing the bandage end with strips of surgical tape.

"Obviously he was told to do it. We were getting too close."

Putting her sock back on, she held it up toward Hunter. "Look what you did, asshole." Wiggling her finger through the hole. "I hate holes in my socks." She put it on and eased her foot back into her boot.

"How do you know it was his chief of staff?"

"He was found in his car hours later. Shot twice in the head. Never got his thirty pieces of silver. Just two pieces of lead... Look at that, I just made a rhyme."

Eve stood with the help of the wall, put some weight on her foot, winced and flinched, gingerly rested on her heel. Leaned her back against the wall to remain standing.

Hunter said, "Enough chit-chat. Let's head to the top, shall we. John, pick up the case. You go first. Eve, you follow.

Eve said, "It'll be slow going."

"We got time. Missile weighs a hundred pounds, right Trahison?"

"Just over."

"So it will be slow going anyway. Move it."

John picked up the case with both hands and leaned against its weight. He stepped over the Lieutenant's body to get to the first of the spiral stairs that ran from the kitchen, where they were standing, to the watch room. The stairs were built on the inside of the lighthouse's outer wall. The stairway walls and ceiling were also covered in white subway tiles.

They made their way up five or six steps when Eve said, "Ok, Trahison, I answered your questions. Your turn. Who else is connected to your uncle? I want names."

"Looks to me like you're in no position to demand anything. And even if I knew names, why the hell would I tell you?"

"Because if you tell me now you'll save yourself a lot of unneeded pain and suffering once we get back to shore."

"Torture? Really? I have rights."

"The Patriot Act says otherwise. The only right you have now is choosing your method of execution. Might I suggest something slow and agonizing. I'd be happy to help."

"I won't be executed. Besides, even if I am, the reason behind all of this still stands. It will all be worth it."

"If by that you mean H.R.7174 becomes law, well, no, that's not gonna' happen either."

John turns toward Hunter. "She's full of shit, right?"

"Afraid not. The bill is dead. And so is this mission."

"Then why are we going ahead with it? I really don't care either way. But why do you want to nuke DC?... Oh... wait... I know what you're doing."

"Just shut up and keep moving."

They were at the second level. John struggled with the weight as he walked three more steps, just past the doorway, and put the case down to rest. Eve, leaning against the wall, hopped up each step. She occasionally placed some weight on her wounded foot's heel, and was keeping pace. Hunter took up the rear. Glock in hand. MP-5 hung on his chest, the strap around the back of his neck.

John continued up the stairs. When they reached the third level, Eve said, "The bill is dead now. There will be no law to establish what amounts to a parallel government. Ever. So there's nothing stopping you from telling me who else was working with your uncle. I know you've never met your fellow turncoat standing behind me here. By the look on your face, you were as surprised as I was when he went all Al Pacino a few minutes ago. So… who else is working with your uncle?"

"What the hell. What have I got to lose?" Gesturing toward Hunter. "He's going to kill us both anyway. Think about it. It's his only logical move. I'm stopped before I rain down more terror. You, well, he'll say I shot you first. At least, that'll be his story. His sad, heartfelt story. Your relationship with him is about to end with another bang, sweetheart. This one will be fatal, I'm afraid."

She knew John was right. At least to a point. She was nearly certain that Hunter was not going to have John shoot the missiles. First, he knows that an array of Patriots at NAS Pax are waiting to spring at the first whiff of rocket fuel.

Besides, he wouldn't unleash such hell on innocent people. Not on his own. Especially now that it would produce zero gain. That much she knew in her gut. The rest was ephemeral. So, apparently, were the last several months, nearly a year, with him. She was feeling an old familiar crust forming around her heart. *It started when the President showed me that transcript.*

John continued. "Never got names. Closest my uncle ever came to telling me who else was involved was a mention of someone else in the Senate, a Supreme Court Justice, and someone close to the President. Don't know who any of them are. Couldn't even begin to guess. I tried. And none of them know about me, either. Designed that way. Safer."

"Safer? For who? More than half a million people thought they were safe in their homes, schools, workplaces and streets! They no longer exist because of you."

"That's a bullshit number. You'll see. One day soon I'll be back in Boston. Once again roaming the wonder-filled exhibit halls of the Museum of Science."

"Nope. Not bullshit. If anything, after all the DNA work is complete, the number of dead will likely be even higher. And the Museum's gone. It's a pile of ash, thanks to you."

John put the case down and sat hard on the tiled step below it. "No way. The museum's gone? You're lying!"

"Why would I lie about that?"

"Shit... Shit! I *loved* that place, man. Loved it. Damn it!"

"Wait. You're telling me that obliterating half a million people doesn't phase you, but destroying the Museum of Science knocks you out of your shoes? You are one fucked up specimen, Trahison. Psych eval we saw doesn't cover the half of it. Must run in the family."

"Fuck you! What do you know?!"

Hunter said, "Enough already! Get up, Trahison. Move. Up those stairs. One more floor. Almost there."

Turning behind her, Eve said, "How do you think you're getting out of this? The President and others already know you're a traitor. Regardless of what happens here, you're still going to prison, or worse."

"Nice of you to worry about me."

"Nope. Not worry. Trust me. Affection turned to disdain in the Oval Office. This is curiosity. You're screwed six ways to Sunday, Hunter. What's your play?"

"Trahison's mostly right. My story today, both tragic and heroic, should buy me enough time and enough empathy to get me to my jet. That's all I need. I'll soon be hurtling off into the night sky. Never to be seen or heard from again. My plan's in place. I'm about to become a ghost."

"You're working with the person close to the President, aren't you?"

Hunter made a quick fake smile. "Get going, hopalong."

She put her hand against the wall, hopped up two more steps, turned toward Hunter and said, "I can't believe I..."

"Believe what? Fell for me?"

She continued hopping. "Never mind... Screw it."

"Falling for me was the hope. But I didn't plan on falling so hard for you."

"Oh, what bullshit!"

"Get close, yes. Report progress, absolutely. But fall in love... no, not part of the plan. And I think you believe me, Eve. Our connection was no act. Not on my part."

She stopped to face him again. "Well, sure! Everyone knows the quickest way to a girl's heart is a bullet in the foot. And *nothing* says 'I love you' like a matching pair of nine mills to the head. Really, what girl wouldn't be swooning right now?... There are no police boats waiting at Hoopersville, are there?"

"Nope."

John stopped. Put the case down and sat. "I need a minute." While Hunter and Eve were still looking at each other, John started rubbing his calf, surreptitiously loosened the bandage around the small Beretta, removed and palmed it. He stood, slipped the gun into his right pants pocket. Picked up the case, went up the last four steps, entered the watch room and put the missile case down in the middle of the floor.

Eve and Hunter followed John into the watch, an eight-foot wide round room surrounded by windows, not just the four that are on every other level. The light from the rotating beam ten feet above them cast continuously revolving and shifting shadows across the floor and walls. On the south side, a door led to a railed metal deck that extended out five feet all the way around the lighthouse. The windows and deck provided an unobstructed three-hundred-and-sixty-degree view, fifty-three feet above the Bay.

Eve said, "You killed Trevor, didn't you."

"After my meeting with Alex. Had to. I drafted him. Supplied the senator's coffee cocktail and fed him a story about you. He thought what he was putting in his boss's coffee was just going to knock him out, incapacitate him so he couldn't talk to you. He didn't know it was lethal. Trevor was easy in, easy out. Plenty of time left over to change clothes and meet you at the restaurant."

John was startled. "*You* killed my uncle? You sonofabitch! What the fuck for!?

"It was unavoidable." Pointing at Eve. "But you really should be blaming her and her tenacity. She got way too close much too quickly."

John just stood there, seething, staring at them both.

Eve continued, "Is Alex part of your cannibalistic cabal?"

"Alex doesn't have a clue." Chuckling. "Cannibalistic?" Saying each letter. "W... T... F?"

A three hundred-foot container ship, taller than the lighthouse, began passing by on the western side, heading south—the ship's lights outlined the entire massive vessel, illuminating thousands of shipping containers covering the entire length and width of the ship, stacked high and tight, like newly unboxed, multi-colored Lego blocks all locked into place.

Eve continued.

"Yes, cannibals. You and your friend here, his uncle, and whoever else is involved didn't just kill half a million people, you *consumed* them. They no longer exist. There are no bodies to bury. But unlike most cannibals, you didn't do it for survival. You did it for something much, much worse... power. All those people are dead because you and these others wanted more power. More control over the rest of us.

"You and your ilk believe you have some sort of God-given mandate to fix what's wrong with our broken country. That you and you alone are the arbiters of truth. And that somehow gives you every right to be judge, jury, and executioner. Sure, we got more than enough fractures and fragments to go around. No doubt. But when human life is so easily discounted, I don't care what your ideology or rationale is. You're nothing more than murderers. Cold-blooded, calculated, mass murderers." Her hand to her ear. "I think I hear Hitler clapping.

"As broken as our democracy may be, to think that annihilating so many of your fellow citizens on such an incomprehensible scale was even an option, even a consideration, is unfathomable. Calling it patriotism is just sick and twisted.

"Claiming these are justifiable, righteous sacrifices is beyond evil. It's nefarious. And perverse. Your plan came straight from the pit of hell. For what? So a few can rule the many? Really? That old chestnut?... There's a reason that always fails.

"The country is built on the opposite foundation. The many rule the few. Three hundred and thirty three-million citizens impact what the five hundred and something members of Congress who represent them should do on their behalf. Using the most powerful weapon on earth... their vote.

"That's where the real power is. It's why attempts at dictatorships in this country fail. Like yours just did. It will always be three hundred and thirty three-million against one. You *can't* win. It's just simple math."

The whirring motor driving the light's rotating turret above them made the ceiling in the watch room hum. A waft of dank, acidic, diesel exhaust came through the slightly open west window—all that remained of the fast-moving container ship.

Hunter gestured with his gun to Eve, pointed to a spot under a southwest-facing window and said, "Nice speech. Take a seat over there. And behave."

Pointing at him. "Open the door, John, and step out with the case." As John picked up the case and stepped through the door, he started whistling Darth Vader's Imperial March. He placed the case on the metal deck near the door. Took four more steps to the railing.

Hunter came up quickly behind him. But John was waiting. He spun to his right, stepping into Hunter, grabbed his gun-hand with his left and shot him with his right. The barely visible Beretta put three thirty-two caliber rounds into Hunter's throat and neck. One of them severed his brain stem. All Trahison had to do was let go.

Hunter's forward momentum sent him over the rail, falling more than fifty feet to the base deck railing below. His body hit the railing, his MP-5 fell inside the railing and his body went to the outside. The gun slipped between two metal balusters, turned, caught, and held in place. The strap, still around Hunter's neck, snapped tight against the railing, leaving him dangling, like a limp scarecrow.

John turned to head back through the door, his gun arm extended. Eve was already up and, wounded foot be damned, ran through the door, leaning forward, throwing everything she had into lifting and shoving the missile case at Trahison just as he fired, hitting Eve in the chest.

It punched her in the left breast. The Kevlar caught the slug. It hurt a lot but didn't slow her forward momentum. John didn't get off a second shot.

The case hit him hard in the knee, slamming his wounded leg into the metal railing, knocking him backwards and completely off balance. Eve was on him with a tried and true disarming move—blocked his arm to her right, got both hands on his gun hand, snapped his wrist inward, forcing John to wince as he let go. The gun now in her hand, leveled directly in his face, inches away. It all took two-and-a-half seconds.

Gesturing with his head toward the missile case beside him, John said, "Don't suppose I could interest you in seeing what these babies can do, could I? I didn't see much of what happened in Boston."

"I already know what they can do. And I've seen more than enough for both of us." She fired the four remaining rounds point blank into his face. Backed up to let him drop to the deck at her feet, along with the gun.

She leaned over the railing. As the light from the beam passed overhead, she saw Hunter's body hanging twenty feet above the choppy Chesapeake swells. She turned and limped back through the door, kept going to the end of the room. She grasped the railing with both hands and hopped up the eight spiral stairs leading to the lantern room, pushed open the hatch door and entered.

Eve shielded her eyes from the blinding light encased in what looked like a four-foot tall, carved, thick angular-cut glass cylinder just two feet away. She turned to find the door, opened it and walked onto the deck to the railing.

Leaning on her elbows, she stood, staring out into the blackness. The light behind her split open the sky in long sweeping arcs, washing over her in waves.

Chapter 58

Eve opened her eyes and for a moment thought she was dreaming. She quickly adjusted to the brightness. The familiar sun-dappled white stone walls, cathedral ceiling ribbed with ancient hand-hewn wood joists, rafters, massive cross beams and lattices at the roof's peak.

The smell of baking bread caused her to sit up, toss the bed covers aside and make her way across the floor, the boot on her left foot not impeding her one iota.

Went past one of her large abstract painting hanging on the wall to the chair in the corner of her room that held her bathrobe. She put it on as she went to the opposite corner, past a steel whale sculpture her grandfather made for her when she was twelve. She reached to the floor and opened a horizontal, pine hatch door and clamored down six steep stairs—more like a ship's ladder—to a landing and then two more stairs to the wide-plank pine living room floor.

She stepped to her left and stood in front of the massive fireplace—it took up an entire wall, from staircase to corner, around which was the open kitchen.

A wood fire crackled and spat on the left side of the cavernous, ancient stone and brick hearth. On the right side firewall of brick, hundreds of years ago, the builder added a bread oven. Behind its closed, arched steel doors wafted the source of Eve's wake-up call.

"Good morning, sleepy head," her grandmother's voice came from the kitchen. Eve went around the corner and walked briskly over to her. She was at the marble countertop kneading a large batch of dough. Her long white hair, folded into a wild bun with a red scrunchie, bobbed in synch with the waddle of flesh under each arm as she pushed, folded, and pounded her fists into the gooey dough. She stopped as Eve hugged her from her side, bent down to kiss her cheek. She leaned her head on her grandmother's shoulder and remained for a minute, "Good morning, Memere." Her grandmother kissed her forehead before resuming her kneading.

"You've been asleep for two days. I thought you might be ready for the fresh bread alarm."

"It never fails. Where is Pepere? I haven't seen him since he picked me up at the airport. I wasn't very talkative. I'm not sure I even thanked him."

"He mentioned that."

"I want to make it up to him. Hang out like we used to. Drink strong coffee and talk about art. He can even smoke a cigar. Hell, I might just smoke one with him."

"He's delivering two of his recent pieces for a group exhibit at the Liza Gallery in Quebec City. They called him a couple of months ago. He's been working like crazy to finish them. Burned his arm pretty good with the welder last week because he was too impatient. He'll be back in another hour or so."

"They called him? Wow! He didn't tell me."

"How could he? You "zoned out," as he put it, for nearly the entire trip back from the airport. And then you went to sleep for two days."

"I know. I'm sorry."

"Don't be silly. We know you went through a lot. We're both just glad you're home. Part of what makes us "*us*" is missing when you're gone."

"I know. Me, too. So you'll be happy to hear I plan to stay a while. Perhaps a long while. I need some time away from Boston."

"So much death. It's all over the news. A Senator? Who would have ever in a million... And you were so close to it, too."

"Very close... Too close."

Just how close is something Eve will never share with her or her grandfather. Although she will likely talk "around" some of this with her grandfather. His Top Secret clearance is still in good standing. And she valued his wise input, but mostly his listening ear. Otherwise, everything that she did, said, saw and heard over the last year simply gets added to the list of things she can't ever talk about. It's a long list. And she realized how much of it is becoming an old list.

She certainly can't talk to her grandparents, or anyone for that matter, about her debriefing with the President. Just the two of them. Her insistence. And he soon discovered why.

President Olson wasted no time and flew into NAS Pax on Marine One. The helicopter landed within the hour of her arrival from the lighthouse. He met her at the hangar where Hunter had parked Homeland's Gulfstream and where Eve could get some medical attention for her foot.

After clearing everyone out of the helicopter, the President and Eve met alone for nearly an hour, where she relayed everything that happened and everything that was said. He stood, thanked her and, uncharacteristically for him, gave her a big hug.

Her foot wound was treated and put in a boot cast by the base doctor. The President arranged for a pilot to take the Gulfstream to wherever Eve wanted to go. She knew instantly where that needed to be. She called her grandmother as the jet taxied onto the runway.

That was four days ago.

Eve continued. "It'll be great. I'll open up my studio. Paint. Read. Hang out with you guys. See my uncles and cousins."

"I love the sound of all of that."

The house phone rang and Eve's grandmother answered. "Hello? Yes, she's here. Who can I tell her is calling. Excuse me?" Looking shocked, befuddled, at a complete loss for words as she held the phone out to Eve and finally managed, "She... she... she said, 'please hold for the President of the United States.'"

Eve took the phone. Her grandmother left the kitchen, went around the corner, stirred the fire, added a fresh log, and sat down on one of the two leather club chairs in front of the fireplace. She wanted to listen, but didn't want to hover.

President Olson said, "So, how's the foot?"

"Fine, thank you, Mr. President. Doc says the cast comes off in a couple weeks and then it's up to me and a lot of walking and running to get it back to normal."

"That's great to hear."

"You didn't call just to ask me about my foot, did you, Mr. President."

"You got me. Here it is. I need you, Eve. I need your help. You know exactly what I need your help with."

"I do, sir, but there are so many other—"

"No. No one else is as capable as you are, Eve. And there's no one I trust more than you. Not with this. Not now… You got us this far and you should see it all the way through. Besides, I don't know who I can and can't trust, Eve. And you know why."

"Yes, sir, I do… Ok. I'm in. Who will I be reporting to?"

"Me. Directly. Now that I know I can trust Alex, thanks to you, I'll probably loop him into some of this. But it's gotta' be just the two of us. At least until we flush out some traitors. Yank some threads. See where they lead. You'll find out. I'll clear it with Wright." She knew he meant the CIA Director, Richard Wright, her boss's boss.

"When do you need me, sir?"

"Well, the news media is in a feeding frenzy now that what the Trahisons did and why they did it has been made public. Anyone else connected to it will go dark. So we can give all that some time to settle. And you need time to heal and rest, Eve. Come see me in eight weeks. Okay?"

"Yes, sir."

"Great. We'll talk soon. On behalf of a grateful nation that will never know who you are or what you did, I thank you, Eve."

"You're welcome, Mr. President." The line clicked silent and Eve hung up the phone.

She stood staring out a large west-facing window. The sun, rising up from behind, created diamonds of light that skipped across the St. Lawrence River, lit up the fields and trees on the opposite bank, and enflamed the distant Laurentian Mountains.

"Memere, I think the bread's done."

Acknowledgements

First, I want to thank my brother, Paul, whose volunteer work restoring the Sandy Neck Lighthouse on Cape Cod prompted me to ask the question: *what if?*

I also want to extend my deepest gratitude to Constance Skedgell for her enthusiastic encouragement and saying out loud the words I had only uttered in my heart, *"You're a novelist."*

And I want to express many thanks to Steve Sherrell, Bob Love, Victor Watts, Bill McGrath, Gary Ricke, James Leslie, Phil Halton, and Chris Cervelloni.

About the Author

After majoring in marketing at Bentley University, Richard spent a career as a copywriter and creative director serving such clients as Red Lobster, Ducati Motorcycles, Marriott Hotels, and Clorox. He also brought his writing skills to bear for communications agencies that serve nonprofit organizations, including American Red Cross, Wounded Warrior Project, Toys for Tots, CARE, Special Olympics and many others. And he was a frequent editorial contributor to *Fundraising Success Magazine.*

In 2000, he helped launch acclaimed author Stephen King's internet publishing debut and the world's first mass-marketed e-book, *Riding the Bullet.* Richard wrote the online ad campaign that prompted more than 400,000 people to purchase and download the novella.

His screenplay, *Graven Image,* placed in the top twenty percent of the Academy of Motion Pictures' Nicholl Fellowships international screenwriting competition in 2014.

Richard is also an accomplished fine art painter. Over the past thirty years, he has exhibited work in numerous solo and group shows. His work was represented by two commercial art galleries in his native Boston and is now represented by a gallery in Chicago, where he currently resides.

Richard and his wife have four adult children and two grandchildren.

Warpath Press is dedicated to publishing the very best in military writing from around the globe.

We believe that writing that is rooted in the human experience of war and conflict, even when written by non-veterans, allows us as a society to examine how human nature responds under extreme pressure. It also gives us a means to ask the big questions about life.

"Military stories" aren't all action-adventure novels. We are committed to finding ways to push the boundaries of "military writing" in new directions, bending it into new shapes that serve society in better ways.

Many of the literary greats of the early to mid-20th century wrote about war and its effects. But Hemingway, Remarque, Dos Passos, Faulkner, Wouk, Greene and Waugh, only had the impact that they did because they were published.

Today, they would likely have been ignored by the major publishers.

And that is why we do what we do.